DOCTO

Sympathy is the last thing the recently widowed Emma Nichols wants when she takes a nurse-receptionist job at a busy health centre. And sympathy is the last thing she gets from Dr Matthew Scofield. In fact, the only emotion they seem to generate is hate! It doesn't take long, though, before Emma realises how easily hate can turn to love . . .

DOCTOR MATTHEW

BY

HAZEL FISHER

MILLS & BOON LIMITED
15–16 BROOK'S MEWS
LONDON W1A 1DR

First published in Great Britain 1984
by Mills & Boon Limited

© Hazel Fisher 1984

Australian copyright 1984
Philippine copyright 1984

ISBN 0 263 74843 X

Set in 11 on 12 pt Linotron Times
03–0984–47,000

Photoset by Rowland Phototypesetting Ltd
Bury St Edmunds, Suffolk
Made and printed in Great Britain by
Richard Clay (The Chaucer Press) Ltd
Bungay, Suffolk

CHAPTER ONE

'THIS IS Dr Matthew's room,' Mrs Ruth Evans said, adding with a smile, 'He's my favourite. Got a soft spot for him, I have!'

Her infectious laugh rang out and Emma Nichols smiled a little. Presumably Dr Matthew was the grey-haired, cuddly-bear type she'd glimpsed earlier. He looked friendly. And she might be glad of a friendly face among the doctors.

It was her first day at the health centre in Calbridge, a busy market town near the south coast. A day she had half-dreaded, half-welcomed. Of course she was only a receptionist-cum-typist. No nursing would be required of her, thank goodness. She didn't think she could cope with that, not yet . . .

Absently, she ran her fingers through her fine, corn-gold hair, her deep blue eyes pensive. She kept her hair short and neat now, having savagely cropped it when her husband was killed almost exactly a year ago. Rather like primitive women chopping off a finger in grief, she reflected. She had wanted to die, too, but somehow kept going, as grey days followed black, wakeful nights.

Eventually she would return to nursing, finish the training she'd given up at Tony's insistence. But not yet. She needed a little more time, she told herself, as she followed Ruth Evans' short, bustling figure. At twenty-six, the prospect of becoming a student again was not particularly inviting.

The health centre was fairly new, Ruth explained. 'Gets all the doctors together. Makes it easier for everyone,' she went on, opening yet another door.

A slightly dazed Emma followed her into a cupboard of a room. 'Tea-room,' Ruth said proudly. 'I expect you could do with a cup. I know *I* could.'

She plugged in the electric kettle and set out mugs while Emma sank gratefully into a shabby fireside chair, its green cover sadly in need of renovation. Despite its smallness, there were three such chairs crammed into the room—plus a couple of equally old pouffes and a rocking-chair.

'That's Mrs Parry's rocking-chair, love. Don't sit in it, whatever you do!' Ruth chuckled, seeing Emma's interest.

'I've one at home, Ruth. Quite an heirloom. It belonged to my great-grandmother.'

Tony's favourite chair, she recalled with a sharp stab as memory returned. She'd tried putting it away, even went so far as to advertise it for sale. But she could not sell it. When eager, would-be buyers called, she'd turned them away. It would be selling part of Tony, and that she could never do.

'My mother still has hers,' Ruth put in, as she handed Emma a colourful mug bearing the portrait of a Muppet. 'That's a spare mug. We each bring our own.'

Emma nodded, murmuring her thanks. She was about to ask more about the health centre activities when the door of the room opened and a very tall, broad-shouldered man walked in, nearly tripping over Emma's long, slender legs which she'd stretched out comfortably in front of her.

Hastily, she tucked them underneath the chair, an apology on her lips. But one icy glance from the stranger, and the words died unsaid.

Rather sleepy-looking, blue-grey eyes swept dispassionately over her, then dismissed her as of no importance. He turned to Ruth Evans, whose pleasant face was wreathed in smiles.

'There you are, then! And wasn't I just talking about you! You'll be wanting a cup.' Without giving him time to reply, she poured hot, strong tea into another Muppet mug and handed it to the man who, to Emma's horror, settled himself in the absent Mrs Parry's rocking-chair.

Seeing a man in a rocking-chair upset her, which was silly because he was nothing like Tony, who had been fair and of smaller build. Older, too.

'Dr Matthew, this is Mrs Emma Nichols. She's helping at reception full-time from tomorrow.'

Dr Matthew's cool gaze lingered on Emma's oval face for a moment, then he nodded.

'I hope you enjoy working here, Mrs Nichols.' His voice was deep, bland. There was nothing in his tone or his expression to which Emma could take serious exception, but nevertheless she felt his hostility. Their legs were only inches apart. His were stretched out in front of him. He had remarkably long legs and she judged him to be well over six foot.

Dr Matthew was handsome, too, with thick, glossy black hair, a slightly Roman nose, high cheek-bones and those candid, big blue-grey eyes under long, dark lashes.

Handsome, and knows it. Emma dismissed him as just a pretty face and continued to sip the scalding tea, listening to the conversation between Ruth and the doctor.

They were discussing someone called Zara. Ruth's daughter, perhaps? Emma knew she had three daughters. Indeed, she'd given Emma a résumé of her life story before the morning had really begun.

'Zara is Dr Matthew's little girl,' Ruth broke in on Emma's thoughts, and she felt a stab of disappointment. Curious that, when she didn't like the man.

Of course, such an attractive man would have been snapped up quite young. His wife was probably an ex-ward sister, Emma decided, as the big doctor drained his mug, patted the motherly Ruth on the head and strode from the room, leaving rather a vacuum.

'There now! What do you think of my Dr Matthew? Isn't he a pet!' Ruth enthused, and her face fell when Emma pointed out that she had seen too little of Dr Matthew to be able to judge, as yet.

'But *everybody* loves him!' Ruth protested, her expression pained. 'Just like his father, he is. The old doctor's retired now,' she explained. 'Dr Matthew didn't want to be a single-handed doctor. Nor did he want to start a new partnership. Sold the old house, he did. Dr Scofield's gone to live with Dr Matthew's sister.'

Emma frowned. 'Who is Dr Scofield?'

'There now! You being a stranger you wouldn't know. Dr Matthew is Matthew Scofield. Because his father was a GP, Matthew came to be called "Dr Matthew" rather than "Dr Scofield Junior". Such a pet lamb, he is!'

By the end of the day Emma was sick and tired of hearing Ruth's opinion of the unfriendly, bear-like Matthew Scofield. Fortunately there were another six doctors at the health centre so she would not be seeing much of him.

This first day Emma wasn't expected to do very much. Apart from the guided tour of the busy centre, she sat in the waiting area with Ruth and observed the routine. Each patient gave his or her name to the receptionist on duty. The receptionist entered the name on a list, then another hurried through to the records section with a duplicate of the list so that the medical records clerk could obtain the necessary medical notes.

Nearly all the doctors had a one-hour surgery in the morning and most had a one and a half hour one in the evening. Those would be Emma's busiest times, the rest of the day being taken up with fixing appointments for the various clinics held there and in typing the few letters the GPs needed to write. The centre employed a full-time medical secretary, but she couldn't cope with all the correspondence, much of it emanating from health visitors and the child guidance section. Emma was being employed mainly for the morning surgeries, at least in the beginning.

The exception to the one-hour morning surgery

rule was Dr Deborah More, the health centre's only lady doctor.

'She has a three-hour surgery on Monday mornings. She likes being different,' Ruth said disparagingly.

'Monday morning is a busy time for doctors, I know,' Emma put in. 'All the ailments of the weekend come to the fore on Mondays!'

'She still likes to be different, that one,' Ruth insisted. 'She sees patients by appointment, too. So does Dr Dutton. Everyone else has a general free-for-all!'

'Including your Dr Matthew?' Emma asked teasingly, and Ruth chuckled.

'Yes. Including my Dr Matthew! A word of warning, though. You must watch out for his wife. She causes trouble sometimes.'

Perplexed, Emma was about to ask in what way she caused trouble, when she felt eyes boring into her. A tall, well-built redhead was frowning at her, and Emma quickly decided this might be Mrs Scofield Junior.

'This is Mrs Nichols, Doctor.' Ruth swiftly made the introductions. 'Dr Deborah More, Emma.'

Dr More offered her hand, her sharp green eyes missing no detail of Emma's appearance which was, Emma knew, decidedly dowdy. She hadn't bothered much since Tony's accident. Evidently her dowdiness won full marks from the attractive redhead though, for she smiled.

At five feet eight, Emma was perhaps an inch taller than the doctor. They both had pale skin and both wore their straight hair cut very short. There the similarity ended. Although Dr More lacked Emma's excellent bone structure, she made the most of what she had. Her make-up was skilfully applied, her eyes enhanced by the clever use of cosmetics, her lips red and luscious. After wishing Emma a happy stay with them, Dr More drifted away on a cloud of expensive perfume and Ruth wrinkled her snub nose in disgust.

'After Dr Matthew, she is. That one means trouble for him. Too fond of the bright lights,' Ruth volunteered, not giving Emma time to mention the mysterious Mrs Scofield.

If Dr Matthew was married he would hardly carry on with another doctor. Apart from being unethical, it was unwise. Emma shrugged the problem away. It was clearly no business of hers.

It was a bitty day. Emma felt she'd achieved nothing at the end of it. She had simply listened and absorbed information, and shown new patients to the chairs outside their particular doctor's surgery. Most of the patients knew the way better than she did!

Swiftly she drew a diagram of the surgery layout, numbering the rooms on her plan. No 1 was Dr Matthew, No 2 was Dr Dutton, No 3 the glamorous Deborah More. The next surgery, tucked away around a corner of the spacious building, was Dr David Rinsler's. Next to him was the Mauritian doctor, and No 6 was Dr Raye. The seventh surgery was up a short flight of stairs, so Emma knew she would remember that one without difficulty. The room belonged to Dr Philip Partington, who was the elderly, grey-haired man she'd seen in the car-park.

The others were, so far, unknown quantities, and Emma felt she would never remember which doctor was which. Only Dr Matthew, Dr More and Dr Partington stood out.

Then there was the clinic staff. Apart from Ruth Evans there was Mrs Parry, who generally did evenings only, plus the two medical records clerks who also did reception duties when required.

'You being a nurse might be useful,' Ruth said thoughtfully as she ushered Emma out of the now silent building. All the doctors had finished their evening surgery and the clinics were closed. A light burned in Dr More's room but, as far as she knew, all the others had left.

'I'm not a nurse, Ruth,' she put in. 'Not really. I did quite a bit of my training after I left secretarial college but I never qualified. I left soon after I got married.'

Before Ruth could reply, a cold voice broke in. 'A dreadful waste, Mrs Nichols. Waste of taxpayers' money, tutors' time and your own life.' Emma's blue eyes darkened with pain as Dr Matthew moved out of the shadows.

'Wasn't I just thinking the same thing!' Ruth exclaimed, and Emma's lips tightened. It was dark now, a January fog hiding her pained expression from them. She was determined they would never know the hurt their words caused.

'I had my reasons for discontinuing training, Doctor,' she said coolly. Then, wishing them both goodnight, she walked briskly away towards her small car. The doctor called after her, but his words were lost in the foggy air as she reached the Mini which was parked on the opposite side of the road.

At least tomorrow was, thank goodness, half day in the town, and the health centre closed at one o'clock. Normally if she helped out at morning surgery she would not have to stay for evening surgery as well, so today had been a strain in more ways than one, she mused as she turned into the small parking space in front of the old, creeper-hung house in Penlow, where she rented a room.

It's as well I don't live in Calbridge, she thought, as she clattered up the worn stairs. I might have landed Dr Matthew as my GP!

The room was big and airy, overlooking the local recreation ground. She had excellent views of the sports in the summer, but now she closed the foggy night out, the rich velvet curtains swishing as she pulled them across.

Everything in the room was of good quality. Items she and Tony had saved for. They had lived in a modern house just outside Worthing. If she'd stayed there, his insurance would have paid off the mortgage and the house would have been hers. Better a whole house than one room, however spacious. But it held too many memories, so she'd sold up, keeping just a few choice pieces of furniture for her new home. The velvet curtains, great-grandmother's rocking-chair, a three-seater convertible sofa, some heirloom glassware.

Wearily she kicked off her sensible, low-heeled shoes and flopped onto the settee. Tonight, for some reason, she avoided the rocking-chair. She could feel the arrogant Dr Matthew's disproving presence.

Who was he to take her to task in that way? How dare he! Tony hated her nursing, disliked the long hours he had to spend alone as she followed the prescribed training—the unsocial hours, night duty, spells in theatre and in casualty. The poor dear needed her and he'd feared for her safety after he'd read about trouble in casualty on Saturday nights when the pubs closed.

Why, he had begged her to leave St Aidan's! Knowing how he hated her being there, how could she have continued?

Leaving was heart-breaking, she recalled. Matron reduced her to tears and the nurse tutors had gazed reproachfully at her, insisting that she must reconsider. All in vain. What Tony wanted, Tony must have—even though she had little more than a year's training left to do. Tony had been her whole life, her reason for living. Although she had parents, Tony became, in a way, an extra parent to her.

For Emma had committed the cardinal sin of falling for a patient. Perhaps, at first, it had been gratitude on Tony's part. Emma's nursing, un-skilled though she was, had helped to pull him through a major operation. For her part, she had been flattered that a much older man of the world like Tony Nichols should fancy her, a gawky, teen-age student nurse. Although he had had his faults and had forced her to give up the job she adored, she hadn't minded at the time. If her darling Tony was happy, so was she. They were happier than other people, including her parents, she'd realised, despite his possessiveness. It was Tony's way of showing how much he cared.

Now, of course, she bitterly regretted the decision to leave nursing. One day she would apply to continue the training. And if, in the meantime, she could occasionally use her nursing skills at the health centre, she would not feel so useless.

Next day Emma awoke refreshed, almost eager for the morning's work—a good sign after so many months of staring into space. She hadn't wasted the months since the accident, though, having had a part-time job in an estate agents. She wanted to get completely away from hospitals for a time. But the job was boring once she'd got the hang of it, the same stereo-typed letter to each vendor and purchaser, similar details of houses on the stencils she'd prepared. She wasn't completely absorbed in the work and it had left her too much time for brooding.

Calbridge Health Centre promised to be a challenge and it brought a sparkle to her eyes as she locked her car door and hurried into the reception area. The centre opened its doors to the public at eight-thirty, though the doctors were not due to start until nine.

Ruth had told her that Dr Matthew, Dr More and Dr Partington usually started seeing patients soon after eight-thirty—depending upon what sort of night they'd had, of course. If they had been out on emergency visits they were often late starting surgery, which meant they would also be late starting their morning rounds. Not for anything would *she* become a doctor! If only the public realised what a difficult time GPs had they might not make so many demands upon them. They . . .

'Good morning, Mrs Nichols.' There was no mistaking Dr Matthew's deep voice and Emma forced a smile to her lips. There was no point in antagonising the man.

She acknowledged his greeting pleasantly. Indeed it *was* a good morning, with yesterday's damp, foggy air seeming no more than a bad dream.

'You're pale,' he went on. 'I hope you are not sickly. The work is demanding.'

'You are very observant, Doctor,' Emma said crisply. 'Perhaps my paleness is due to lack of make-up. I don't wear any.'

He raised a shaggy brow. 'Why not? Still in mourning, perhaps?' he suggested, and Emma flushed.

The effort of keeping a close guard on her tongue was too much and her eyes flashed blue fire back at him. 'That was a personal question! As long as I carry out my duties does it matter how dowdy I am?'

He shrugged immense shoulders, the faintest of smiles crossing his wide mouth. 'You're aware you are dowdy, then?'

Before Emma could retaliate, the doctor disappeared through the side-door, and she forced herself to contain her fury. He was a pig! A swine! He had no right to speak like that. Still fuming, she almost didn't see Ruth Evans, who was unwrapping yards of red scarf from around her neck.

'Saw you through the window,' Ruth said

cheerily. 'Talking to my Dr Matthew! What was he saying?'

It was impossible to take offence at Ruth's inquisitiveness, and Emma gave her a résumé of the conversation.

'That isn't like him!' Ruth exclaimed, her dark eyes widening. 'Must have been *her*. Playing up, I shouldn't wonder.'

'If "her" means Mrs Scofield, you had better tell me in what way she plays up,' Emma insisted, but Ruth seemed reluctant to say more.

'I don't like to talk about the woman. I pity her, really.'

'If she's married to that arrogant, interfering so-and-so, then I pity her, too!' Emma said sharply, wishing Dr Matthew and his wife light-years away from Calbridge!

Morning surgery was busy. Dr Matthew started promptly at eight-thirty, most of the others beginning just before nine. Emma was introduced briefly to the other doctors before surgery, committing to memory their faces and general characteristics, hoping she wouldn't get them mixed-up.

Stephen Dutton bore a superficial resemblance to her darling Tony, so she would not forget him. David Rinsler was very young and keen, looking hardly old enough to be qualified. Mahmoud Bhunjun was a quiet, bespectacled Mauritian, and Alan Raye was a dour, balding man. Dr More and Dr Partington she'd already met. As for Dr Matthew Scofield, there was no likelihood of her not remembering him!

It wasn't long before she had another confronta-

tion with the wretched man. Because he was ready
to begin surgery almost before the main doors were
opened, there were, naturally enough, no record
cards to post through the letter-box chute leading
from the corridor to his surgery.

Unfairly, he blamed Emma for this. 'Why don't I
have any medical records yet?' he demanded, startling Emma by coming up behind her. For some
reason, the queue which always formed outside the
centre was only a short one and Ruth had dealt with
them promptly, giving Emma the duplicate list to
take to medical records.

The clerk was busy at the counter, the other one
being off sick, so Emma was faced with the daunting task of finding the appropriate records. And
having two Smiths and a Brown on the list didn't
help.

Angrily she turned, almost colliding with him. 'I
haven't found all the folders yet, Doctor. And
there are two Smiths, J. on the list and I can't see
which one is yours.'

She blinked back tears of frustration as Dr
Matthew moved her none too gently to one side.
'Let me look. I'm only here until ten,' he said
bitingly.

Emma choked back the hasty retort that
trembled on her lips, even managing to meet his
blue-grey gaze as he waved the record cards at her.

'Always get their full forenames, Mrs Nichols. In
the case of a common name it could save a lot of
valuable time. *My* valuable time,' he emphasised.

'Yes, of course, Doctor,' Emma murmured before resuming her search for some notes for Dr

More. She certainly did not intend apologising to the man. She was new. Couldn't he make allowances for her?

It seemed he could not, for as soon as his surgery had finished he was on the intercom asking for her to take some dictation.

Knowing she would be blamed for any minor fault made her nervous, and she dropped her note-pad on the floor of his surgery as she entered. It clattered on the vinyl tiles and Dr Matthew glowered at her, his shaggy black brows meeting in the middle, lending him a ferocious look.

'I'm sorry, Doctor,' Emma said quietly, bending to retrieve the notebook at the same time as he did. Only by a fraction did their heads avoid a hasty collision, and a flushed and embarrassed Emma took the pad from him with hands that trembled.

In some ways he reminded her of her old sister tutor. Everyone trembled in *her* presence, too!

She met his mocking gaze as he helped her to her feet. 'I hope you aren't always so careless, Mrs Nichols,' he said tightly. 'Accidents don't happen. They're caused.'

'Carelessness costs lives!' She threw back another slogan at him, and a brief smile tugged at his mouth.

'*Touché*, Mrs Nichols. Who knows? You might even tame me!'

'That would be impossible,' she snapped, her nerve cracking as he continued to stare. She sat on the hard chair in front of his big desk, waiting for him to begin dictating. Her hands were shaking and she didn't think she would be able to do shorthand, not if he kept staring. His big, sleepy-looking eyes were assessing her, finding fault with her appearance, probably.

She knew she was neat and tidy in her navy jumper and grey skirt. She'd discarded the pink overall she wore during her reception duties. She wore no make-up, no jewellery of any kind other than her wedding-ring of thick, plain gold.

If he didn't like looking at neat and tidy women it was just too bad. Her determined chin lifted a fraction, and the bear-like doctor leaned back in his chair and laughed. Actually laughed at her!

Incensed, Emma sat like a statue, her burning face the only sign of what was going on inside her. White teeth gleamed in his dark-complexioned face and his eyes were full of laughter as they observed her flushes.

Inconsequentially, she noticed the little curl that dangled just over his right eye. A curl so precise that she decided he probably slept with a curler in it! At that moment he ran long, capable fingers through his thick black hair and the curl remained undisturbed, which pleased Emma. She'd found his vice—vanity! It was a wonder he didn't perm his hair, the way some footballers did. She wouldn't put it past him.

Without a word of apology he dropped his eyes to the papers in front of him and began dictating, leaving a nonplussed Emma to catch up with him as best she could. It was a letter to the local hospital about one of his patients, the Mr J. Smith whose name had already caused her enough difficulty.

Because the letter mentioned medical terms the

shorthand outlines required a bit of thought, but Dr Matthew gave her no time to think, no pause while she turned the pages of the notebook. He had a clear idea of what he wanted to say and was visibly annoyed when Emma stopped the flow of words to ask him to repeat a particular phrase.

'It's a medical expression, Mrs Nichols,' he said with exaggerated patience. '*Asteatosis*. It's lack of sebaceous secretion in layman's terms,' he added, scribbling the word down on his pad. 'Here. I've spelled it for you.'

'Thank you,' Emma said crisply, refusing to be browbeaten. If all the doctors were as hateful as he was, she wouldn't be stopping long. She did not need work that badly.

He must have divined her thoughts, for his lip curled as he said scornfully, 'Not giving up yet, are you? I suppose you gave up nursing at the first sign of difficulty? What was it? Too many bedpans to empty? Nursing not the glamorous life you expected?' he went on relentlessly, and Emma jumped to her feet in indignation.

'It isn't any of your business why I left! Though if you must know, it was because my husband asked me to! I loved him more than I love nursing, Dr Matthew,' she finished more calmly, pleased to see she had discomfited him. 'If your marriage is as happy as mine was then you are indeed blessed, Doctor,' she added, while he sat there, stony-faced. 'As it is, I pity your wife!'

As soon as the words were out, Emma wished she could withdraw them. She hadn't meant to hurt the man. It was so unlike her.

'Most people pity my wife, Mrs Nichols,' Dr Matthew said quietly, closing his notepad and walking out. Emma stood by his desk, horror-struck at what she'd said, and at his reply.

Most people pity my wife. His words echoed in the room. At that moment she pitied Matthew Scofield.

CHAPTER TWO

THE REST of the morning passed quickly. Emma typed Dr Matthew's letter and several for Dr Partington and after that she helped out at the chiropody clinic.

But her unkind remarks to Dr Matthew preyed on her mind and it was a miserable, worried Emma who drove slowly home to Penlow. She was finished for the day but he would still be working. Although it was officially a half day for all the doctors, naturally one had to be on call. This afternoon it was Dr Bhunjun's turn, but that didn't mean Matthew was idle. He had patients to visit before he could go home for his lunch.

Home. Just what sort of home did he have? Emma wondered what sort of home life he had, as well. Out of curiosity she had looked up his address. He lived in Calbridge, on the outskirts.

Obeying an impulse, Emma turned the car and headed back towards the market town. She would drive past, just to see what sort of house he had. That she might also see the burly Dr Matthew she put from her mind. She didn't want to see him.

As she might have expected, it was a big house. It was set well back from the road, guarded by five-bar wooden gates. She saw the name King's House as she drove slowly past. An appropriate name for such a vain man, she mused scornfully.

She thought she saw a figure in the long front garden beyond the gates, but wasn't sure, and the traffic was too heavy for her to do more than take a quick peek. It could be Dr Matthew, though he was probably still doing his rounds. Perhaps it was his daughter, Zara.

A little sigh escaped her as she drew up in front of the house where she lived. A daughter. How she wanted one! Tony had liked children but was adamant that Emma wasn't going to have a baby.

He'd felt that children drove a wedge between husband and wife, while Emma thought they cemented a relationship, completed the family unit. Perhaps, being some years older than Emma, he had good reason for not wanting to start a family. As always, she had fallen in with his wishes.

Many times since his death she'd wished she had not. She could have had Tony's child, something tangible to remember him by. What did she have now? Only the ancient rocking-chair he'd loved so much.

In her torment, Emma gave it a kick as soon as she closed the door of her bed-sitter, then was immediately contrite. Ashamed of her outburst of temper, she smoothed its big scarlet cushion, then patted the chair as if in apology.

If you aren't careful, my girl, you will end up talking to that darned chair! she rebuked herself as she gazed without interest at the contents of the small fridge in the dining area of the huge room.

Nothing appealed. There was some ham and she supposed she could make a salad of sorts, but it was too cold. She needed a hot meal.

Turning to her store-cupboard, which was sandwiched between the cooker and the fridge, she found a tin of baked beans she'd forgotten about. Beans on toast didn't appeal either, but it would warm her up a little.

The house was centrally-heated, at least, and Emma leaned gratefully against the radiator. Like the rest of the house, the heating system was years old and often during the night she would lie awake and listen to the clanking of the pipes and radiators. It reminded her of the hospital in which she'd done part of her training. It, too, was ancient, a former Victorian workhouse.

She really ought to take up nursing again. Pensively she gazed at the tin of baked beans, her mind far from the old house. In her thoughts, she was back at the hospital, neat in her blue-striped dress and the cap with its two wide blue bands indicating her second-year status.

Why, oh why, did she give it up? It was too easy, too glib to say that she did it for Tony. Surely she could have talked him round, persuaded him that a year wasn't forever?

Tears streamed down her face and she brushed them away as they fell. She had no time for women who burst into tears whenever the going got tough. She would survive. She had to.

Late afternoon found her in her car once again. Although it was early closing day in most of Calbridge, the shops in Penlow were open and she needed to replenish her stock of food—though she took little interest in meals these days.

There was a supermarket in Penlow and she wheeled the trolley around the store, her mind only half on what she was doing. When she bumped her trolley up against someone's legs she was full of apologies. She really ought to keep her mind on the task in hand. She could have hurt some old lady. But the legs belonged to a man. Dr Matthew.

They stared at each other for a few seconds and Emma stopped apologising. He would believe she'd knocked against him deliberately. Whatever she said or did would be wrong, she felt.

Dr Matthew graciously inclined his head to acknowledge her and Emma felt like striking him. The man brought out a side of her nature that had hitherto lain dormant. She would not have believed herself capable of such strong dislike.

Having done all the apologising she was going to, she turned away, intent on getting to the check-out before the doctor. His trolley was well-loaded, whereas she still had further purchases to make. No matter, she would finish her shopping another day. She had to get away from him. Why, she could not say. It was simply a feeling.

But before she could manoeuvre her trolley out of his way, a girl's voice piped up. 'Is that everything, Daddy? Did you get the bread?'

Emma stopped, her blue eyes intent as the girl came into view. This must be Zara, unless he had another daughter. She had envisaged a child of about six or seven, somehow, but this dark-haired girl was tall and looked about thirteen.

Aware that she was staring, Emma slipped by

and trundled away as quickly as she could to the check-out. Only when she got outside the store did she relax.

She had parked in the supermarket's own car-park and now she saw the doctor's car, a metallic blue Rover, parked nearby. She must get away before they came out.

Quickly, she stowed her shopping in the boot, but she still had to return the trolley to the stand just outside the door. They were coming out with their full trolley as she replaced hers, but she pretended not to notice them. One meeting was enough.

She was sitting in the safety of her Mini, preparing to pull away, when Dr Matthew's daughter came running up to her, long hair flying in the strong wind. Emma frowned, wondering what she wanted. Her nerves were on edge and she couldn't face *any* company, let alone his.

'Please come! Daddy says you're a nurse!' the girl cried, when Emma had reluctantly wound down the window.

'Well, not exactly. It's been a long time,' Emma began, but the girl jumped up and down in agitation and Emma hurried now, believing the doctor had tripped and fallen without her seeing him.

Whatever she thought of the man, she still remembered her first aid and would help him if she could. Quickly Emma followed the girl, seeing that a crowd was gathering at the other exit which had been hidden from her view.

The doctor's daughter swiftly made a passage for them through the crowd, telling everyone she'd brought a nurse, and an embarrassed Emma hurried to Dr Matthew, who was kneeling by the side of an elderly woman. Her relief at finding him unhurt surprised her, but then there was no more time for personal thoughts as she joined him beside the woman.

'Slight concussion. She fell and struck her head,' he said succinctly, and Emma felt like weeping when she saw the old lady's head.

The scalp had a very good blood supply and Emma knew head wounds often appeared much worse than they were because of the amount of blood. Even so, it looked serious and she gently held the pad to the woman's scalp while Dr Matthew searched for other injuries.

The resourceful Miss Scofield shooed away all the onlookers except for an old man who said he was a neighbour of the casualty. An assistant had already dialled for an ambulance and Emma heard its welcome bell as she spoke soothingly to the woman

'Her name's Mrs Walker. She lives on her own,' the man quavered. 'All alone, honest she does, Nurse. Ain't none of her daughters cares about her.'

Emma stifled a sigh. The elderly were too often abandoned by relatives once they had outlived their usefulness. She'd seen it in the geriatric wards. No one visited until the old person was dying or dead, then relatives arrived by the carload, eager to collect anything of value. But that, she realised suddenly, was where she could come in useful. Visiting elderly people like Mrs Walker would help to ease two lots of loneliness—hers and theirs.

She went in the ambulance with Mrs Walker, who, though dazed, was now fully conscious. The general hospital wasn't far and Emma knew she could easily get a bus back to the supermarket to pick up her car. Dr Matthew followed in the Rover together with his daughter and the old man, Mr Wootton, who wanted to see his neighbour settled in. Dr Matthew disappeared with Mrs Walker when they arrived at the A and E entrance of the hospital, and Emma found herself chatting to his daughter, who seemed very straightforward. Her name was Zara Scofield, she informed Emma and Mr Wootton, and she was going to become a doctor like her father, she thought. She wasn't really sure, though, and Emma smiled.

'You can leave the decision a while, can't you? Do you have to choose your special subjects yet?'

'No, but I ought to make up my mind,' Zara said with a frown. 'Daddy says I dither about just like Mother did.'

Emma's eyes flew open. 'Did? I thought . . .' Emma stopped in confusion. It wasn't her business and the child might report the conversation to her father.

'She probably still dithers, but they live apart,' Zara said, matter of factly. Emma silently absorbed the information . . .

Eagerly she breathed in the sights and smells of the hospital, something stirring in her blood as she watched nurses scurrying along, running but seeming only to walk, a trick soon learned! Oh, how she wanted to get back! Even the ubiquitous bedpan round would be welcome. She promised herself she would never grumble about nursing as she'd done in the past, moaning about the unsocial hours, the back-breaking work, over-strict ward sisters . . .

'If you two are finished, we'll get back.' Dr Matthew's voice broke in on Emma's dreams for her future and she flashed him a brilliant smile, her eyes sparkling at the thought of returning to nursing.

He stepped back as if struck, and Emma blushed. She could well imagine what he was thinking of her. She was unaware how beautiful she was when she smiled, how her deep blue eyes sparkled like precious sapphires, how her generous mouth curved invitingly. She believed Dr Matthew saw only the rather drab outfit and the pretty but dowdy widow who, for some reason, he disliked.

'Yes. I'm finished, Doctor,' she said crisply, pulling herself together as she felt his eyes boring into her. 'I'll see you tomorrow.'

Without giving him a chance to reply Emma hurried out, anxious yet again to leave his disturbing presence. It was sleeting and she turned up the collar of her old sheepskin jacket. She hoped the bus wouldn't be long, for there were no taxis in sight.

To phone for one meant going back into the hospital vestibule, and then the arrogant Matthew Scofield might think she was hanging about for a lift from him. That was something she could well do without!

There was a telephone-box on the other side of the road, but it meant taking a chance and dodging the busy traffic, the zebra crossing being some way off. With darkness falling and the sleet reducing visibility, Emma wasn't prepared to take the risk.

Resolutely, she put her head down and walked to the bus-stop which was in the hospital grounds. There was bound to be a bus sooner or later, and meanwhile she could shelter.

But the shelter was full and a dismayed Emma was exposed to the driving sleet as she waited. Then, someone touched her arm. Zara Scofield was plucking at her sleeve, pointing back towards the hospital entrance.

Emma turned reluctantly, not wanting to accept a lift from the man she'd been so rude to that morning—but there was no virtue in catching a chill while she waited for the bus.

Matthew was sitting in his car, the engine purring, and Emma was glad to see Mr Wootton there, too. Zara sat in front with her father and a soaked and chilled Emma sat behind with the old man.

The doctor dropped Mr Wootton off first, then carried on in the direction of Calbridge. Emma bit her lip, unwilling to upset him further by telling him she lived in the opposite direction. It didn't matter. She could certainly get a taxi in Calbridge.

She sneezed, trying to stifle the sound, and Zara clucked sympathetically. 'You mustn't catch cold, Nurse. Daddy was saying how much they rely on you.'

A startled Emma sat upright, her mouth open in disbelief. Then she saw the back of Dr Matthew's neck redden. He must have made some snide remark about her, and his daughter had taken it at face value!

'I didn't know I was so valuable, Zara.' With an effort she kept the anger out of her voice. Ingenuously the girl went on. 'You must be valuable. Daddy said he didn't know how the health centre had managed to run without you! He was telling Mrs Evans. Weren't you, Daddy?'

Emma enjoyed the sudden silence and hoped he was well and truly embarrassed. She would make him eat his words if it was the last thing she did!

He managed to extricate himself nicely by assuring Zara that he thought highly of Mrs Nichols. Emma squirmed, wishing she could give him a piece of her mind there and then. For the moment he was safe, though.

'Home again, here we are,' Zara chanted and Emma opened her mouth, then closed it, as she gazed around her. Zara got out to open the double gates of King's House and a perplexed Emma allowed herself to be driven right up to the front door.

Perhaps she was supposed to get a taxi from there? Annoyed, she sneezed again, then got out of the car, glad to see that the sleet had stopped.

'Come into the house, Mrs Nichols,' Dr Matthew ordered, gripping Emma's arm and almost dragging her indoors. Beyond caring now, Emma found herself passing through a big, high-ceilinged hall and then she was in the sitting-room, her jacket being eased gently off.

'Get yourself warmed up!' the doctor barked as

though it was her fault she was chilled. Resentfully she did so, getting as close to the big log fire as she dared.

This was bliss! If she had a cup of hot, milky coffee she would believe herself in heaven. Hunger began to attack her as she gazed into the sputtering fire, and she longed to see chestnuts roasting there. Or, better still, hot teacakes dripping with butter and honey.

She licked her lips, almost tasting the food. It must be the exceptionally cold day. It was the first time since Tony's accident that she'd taken more than a passing interest in food.

'Tea and some kind of sandwiches are on their way.' Emma jumped, unaware of the doctor's approach until he spoke.

'You must have read my mind!' she smiled. 'I was dreaming of roast chestnuts and toasted teacakes!'

'It's years since I had a chestnut,' Dr Matthew said softly, bending down to warm his hands at the fire.

His back was half turned and Emma could watch him unobserved. He had big, square hands, the nails clean and cut straight across. Capable hands. Healing hands. A strange sensation came over her, and for one mad moment she longed to reach out and clasp them, feel their warmth flow through to her.

She shook herself, alarmed at the train of her thoughts. By wishing for closer physical contact with Dr Matthew she was being unfaithful to Tony's memory. Not putting him first was something he would never forgive.

But he's gone, a voice cried inside her. He's gone and you have to go on living!

She must have uttered some sound, a little sigh perhaps, for the big, burly doctor rose and gazed down at her, his expression inscrutable. His eyes were dark with some emotion. Pity, maybe. Or annoyance because he felt he had to dry out the unwanted new receptionist.

She got up, deciding that to stay longer would be unwise. 'I won't stay for tea, thank you, Doctor. I'm much warmer now.'

He shrugged, evidently uncaring. 'As you wish. I'll drive you back.'

'Oh, no! No, *please*. There's no need,' she cried. Being taken home by him would be worse than sitting by his fire. In any case, she still had to collect her car from the supermarket. 'I'll get a taxi. If I might use your phone?'

His lips tightened. Then he strode from the room and an uncertain Emma followed. He pointed to the smart black and gold wall-telephone in the hall, and nervously she thanked him. A list of numbers was below the telephone and she rang for her taxi, all the while conscious of the doctor's eyes upon her.

He lounged in the doorway, his dark grey suit jacket dangling from one hand, his tie undone, white shirt open at the neck. She could see him plainly out of the corner of her eye and wished him many miles away.

She put her jacket on, unnerved by his silent, somehow accusing presence. Why on earth didn't he move? Was he afraid she was going to use his precious phone again?

She licked her dry lips, wondering how she was going to get past him. She could hardly wait in the hall for the taxi. Then she recalled his daughter's words.

'I'm sorry if you feel I'm an unnecessary addition to the staff, Doctor,' she said stiffly.

He raised an eyebrow. 'Are you unnecessary?'

'You implied as much. Your daughter took your remark about me as a compliment. It certainly could not have been,' she pointed out, tightly.

He inclined his head, those deep-set eyes on her. 'No. It wasn't a compliment. I've no time for people who dabble in whatever takes their fancy,' he said flatly, and Emma began to protest.

Then a car tooted outside and the bitter words remained unsaid. She sent him what she hoped was a cool, disdainful look, then hurried out to the waiting cab.

She loathed the man! Simple dislike had turned within seconds to hatred. How dare he! Who was he to sit in judgment on a fellow human being? Why, he couldn't even make his wife happy! He was only half a man. An unfeeling, uncaring machine whose only concern was his own comfort, his own welfare. She simply could not go on working with him at the health centre.

By next morning some of her anger had evaporated. She could not pretend to like the man, but it should not be too difficult to keep out of his way, she decided.

She'd thought a lot about Mrs Walker. And Mr Wootton. The first opportunity she got, she questioned the health visitor, Mrs Smith, about a visiting service for the elderly.

'We haven't one, as such,' the health visitor admitted. 'There are so many old people here, Emma. The voluntary organisations take care of that sort of thing but there must be many who escape the net.'

Emma eyed her thoughtfully. 'Could I visit some of the old people on the doctors' lists?'

The grey-haired health visitor showed her surprise. 'You really ought to offer your services to the voluntary people. I'll speak to Dr Partington, though,' she promised, and with that a disappointed Emma had to be content.

If she had to join a voluntary visiting service then she would do so. But somehow she felt that visiting some of those on the health centre lists would be more valuable, a chance to get to know the patients better.

Although it would take ages to get to know the patients, she had already begun to make contact. During the morning surgery one or two patients asked about other services available at the centre. And an elderly patient of Dr Matthew, Mrs Huggett, told Emma a good part of her life story.

Mrs Huggett sat at the front of the waiting area. Rows of benches stretched back to the rear door, which led to the annexe where the midwives and others held various classes. During a lull in what was proving to be a busy morning, Mrs Huggett leaned forward and beckoned to Emma. Amused,

Emma sat by the woman's side, happy to chat for a few moments more, though she thought she had heard all Mrs Huggett had to say.

'It's my leg, Nurse,' Mrs Huggett confided, lifting her longish woollen skirt and rolling down her stocking to display a nasty ulcer.

Emma frowned. 'Has the doctor seen it before?'

Mrs Huggett looked affronted. 'I never bother Dr Matthew unless I have to. I've only come now because my grand-daughter insisted. Interfering young madam she is!'

'She was right to insist, Mrs Huggett,' Emma said firmly. 'You should have come before. Dr Matthew won't be pleased that you've left it so long.'

'Oh! Is it bad?' Mrs Huggett whispered, and Emma patted her arm reassuringly.

'It's nothing Dr Matthew can't put right. He will . . . Oh—I must go now.' To her horror, Dr More's tall, shapely figure had appeared in the doorway and she stood, tapping her foot impatiently as Emma hurried over.

'Where is my next patient, Mrs Nichols? I've dealt with the two who were sitting outside my surgery.'

Emma flushed. Dr More was a quicker worker than she'd thought. Even so, the fault was Emma's for not checking.

'I'm sorry, Dr More. I'll call the next one.' Her face still heated, Emma glanced down the list. 'It's a Mrs Green,' she murmured. 'Mrs Green for Dr More,' she called out, but there was no response.

'Get the next one, then!' Deborah More snapped. White coat flying, she hurried back to her surgery and Emma sent in the next patient, then made sure that two more were sitting outside the surgery ready.

Mrs Green turned up a few minutes later, having been shopping. Now Emma could see the squiggle next to Mrs Green's name. Presumably she was intended to translate it into something meaningful! This was something that often happened, but usually with doctors who didn't have an appointment system. The patients could ask the receptionist how far down the list they were and then, if there seemed time, they could go shopping or pop out to the library and still be back in time to be seen. Mrs Green had sadly misjudged the situation.

'Dr More was waiting for a patient, Mrs Green, so I had to show someone else in,' Emma explained to the obese, disgruntled woman.

'I'll sit outside, then.' Before Emma could stop her, Mrs Green had stumped off to the corridor, presumably to sit on one of the patients who were already there!

Distractedly, Emma ran her fingers through her corn-gold hair. Problems, problems. Dr More would be quick to complain to Matthew, she knew. And Matthew would be more than delighted to air his views on the ineffectual Mrs Emma Nichols.

Determined not to give the doctors further cause for complaint, Emma checked regularly to see that there were no empty chairs outside the surgeries. In addition, she had to check in patients, then hurry out with the list of names.

Ruth Evans worked only part-time, Wednesday being her day off, and Emma was having to cope on her own. It was hardly fair on a newcomer. Rather like her experience of being the new girl on a hospital ward and being expected to know all the patients and their treatments by the second day.

Somehow, she coped, though by the end of the morning surgery she felt whacked. She would have a break directly after lunch, but then she'd have to come back to take evening surgery with Mrs Parry. She didn't know if she would have the energy to return!

After the last patient was ushered our she made elevenses for the doctors, leaving the medical records clerk to wheel the trolley in. The doctors and nurses had their own tea-room, the tiny one Emma used being only for the receptionists and secretaries. She'd seen Dr Matthew there that first morning, but realised now he'd popped in because of Ruth Evans. Her younger daughter and Zara Scofield were friends and, from what Emma had gathered, the doctor leaned on Ruth a lot for advice about bringing up his daughter. Presumably the absent Mrs Scofield did not bother with such things.

It upset Emma to think that Zara's mother didn't want her. The girl seemed quite charming, polite and reasonably clean, though untidy! Intelligent, too. How could her mother simply abandon her to the care of her father? Even as a doctor he could not be expected to know everything about children. Coping with a daughter tottering on the brink of womanhood must be a daunting task for the man. No wonder he was so sharp sometimes!

Dr Partington rang for her before he went out on his rounds. Emma had almost forgotten her conversation with the health visitor and assumed the elderly GP had a few letters to dictate—something the doctors generally did just before evening surgery or straight after lunch.

Dr Matthew was with Dr Partington, and Emma's heart sank when she entered the surgery. Dr Partington waved Emma to a seat and she sat down on the comfortable old chair, notebook cradled against her chest.

She and Dr Matthew exchanged cool glances. A very cool glance on her part.

'Dr Partington tells me you want to visit some of the old folk on our lists,' he began gently, and a startled Emma stammered out that she did.

She was expecting verbal blows, not this soft-voiced interest. It could only be a ploy for Dr Partington's benefit. Make the old doctor believe Matthew was really interested in the idea.

Matthew's next words surprised her even more. 'I think it an excellent idea, Mrs Nichols,' he said with the hint of a smile, and Emma eyed him doubtfully.

She didn't trust him an inch. There was a snag in this somewhere and she must find it before the idea snowballed.

'Have you any particular patients in mind, Dr Matthew?' she asked carefully, letting him see that she mistrusted his motives.

'One or two. It would have to be with their permission, of course. And you must liaise with the health visitors,' he warned.

Emma nodded obediently. 'What about the voluntary visitors?'

Dr Partington laughed. 'They have their hands full, m'dear. They will probably be only too pleased. Matthew knows their organiser.'

'Yes. I'll have a word in her ear,' Matthew assured him and Emma nibbled her lower lip anxiously.

It was too good to be true. She had expected anything but this. Could it be that she had picked a project close to Matthew's heart? Maybe he, too, was concerned with the plight of his older patients, particularly those who lived alone. It might be that this project would cause him to be less critical of her. If he was expecting her to give it up after a week or two he would not go to such trouble. Getting the visiting started and then having Emma drop the idea would annoy and confuse the patients.

No, he must be genuinely keen to see the scheme work. Emma's face broke into a delighted smile at the thought. If she and Dr Matthew could work together in harmony, she would be happy for the first time since Tony's accident.

The shrilling of the telephone ended what had become an awkward, pregnant silence, as Matthew stared at Emma, his blue-grey eyes on her face as she smiled. Aware of his scrutiny, she stopped smiling, her face taking on an appealing pink tinge as he continued to watch her.

Dr Partington answered the telephone, seemingly oblivious to the silent drama being played out in front of him. 'It's for you, Matthew. Your father-in-law.'

Emma's eyes darkened with a pain she did not

understand, a longing she could not fathom. His father-in-law. His wife's father. Matthew had a wife and she *must* remember that.

Yet it is irrelevant, she told herself. His status had nothing to do with the project. It shouldn't make a scrap of difference to their professional relationship. But somehow it did.

After a few terse words on the telephone, Matthew put down the receiver, muttered, 'Celia,' to his colleague, then strode from the room.

Emma raised her expressive eyes to Dr Partington, who shrugged. 'Celia is his wife. Sounds as if she's causing trouble again.'

Emma's lips formed into an O but she did not speak.

CHAPTER THREE

CELIA SCOFIELD wasn't causing trouble, as Dr Partington had wrongly prophesied. She would never cause trouble again, for the phone call brought news of a car crash.

She was dead by the time the rescuers pulled her from the wreckage. The driver, a man friend, died later that day in hospital, Ruth Evans informed Emma the following morning. Emma and Ruth were on duty together.

'Oh, Ruth! How awful for him,' Emma murmured, stunned by the news. 'Awful for Zara, too. Have you seen her?'

'She's a hard one, that,' Ruth said disapprovingly. 'She said how sorry she was to hear about the accident but she didn't seem to care a lot.'

'If her mother deserted her, I suppose she has had to bottle up her emotions,' Emma said gently. 'Try to present a hard-as-nails image to the world. Pretend she hadn't been hurt while all the time the wound has been festering.'

'Yes, I suppose so. I really didn't think about it,' Ruth acknowledged. 'She has always seemed so normal, self-contained, like. I never thought about her being disturbed by it all.'

'Did . . . Have they been parted long?' Emma ventured.

'About two years, I should reckon. Perhaps not

that. Mrs Scofield used to come in, though, on some pretext or other,' Ruth explained. 'That's why I said to be wary of her. She had a nasty, spiteful tongue on her. But, there! I mustn't speak ill of the dead. I hope she's found rest now, poor woman.'

Emma wanted to ask how Matthew was taking it, but didn't dare. She found out how he was the following day. It was Friday at last and she would not have to work on the Saturday, Ruth being rostered for that morning.

Matthew summoned Emma to his surgery when the morning rush was over. A trifle nervously, she knocked on his door, wondering how he would appear. Would the tragic accident make him even more unapproachable, or was it a relief to him? Ruth had told her that she believed he still loved Celia, despite all that had passed between them. He hadn't divorced her.

Thanks to the loquacious Ruth, Emma knew that the Scofields had parted and gone back together twice, for the sake of Zara. Then the heavy-drinking, flirtatious Celia had disappeared again and Matthew had banned her from the house because of the disturbance it caused their daughter.

A grim-faced Matthew glanced up as Emma approached him warily. 'About your visiting. There's a Mrs Drummond you can visit whenever you like. I've seen her this morning and told her about you.'

Surprised, Emma murmured her thanks. She felt awkward, not knowing what to say about his wife, not knowing if she should mention the accident at all.

'Here. That's her address and I've written you a note. She probably won't read it but she'll recognise my signature.' Briskly, he tore off the page from his notebook and handed it over.

Their fingers touched momentarily and Emma almost snatched the note from him, eager to be away. At the door she turned, expressive eyes on his face, already prepared for flight if he shouted at her. 'I'm very sorry, Dr Matthew. About the accident and your . . . your wife, I mean.'

Without waiting for any comment she edged out of the room, knowing that he would find fault with her remark. She didn't want there to be any acrimony between them. Not just yet, while he was recovering from the shock. Later, they would probably resume their chilly relationship, but in the meantime she would creep about and try not to antagonise the poor man.

Zara called at the centre just before they closed for lunch. Emma saw her pause in the doorway, presumably looking for her father. Emma beckoned and smiled and Zara came over to her.

'Hello, Zara! I don't think your father is here. Still on his rounds, I expect.'

Zara shrugged as if not bothered either way. She wasn't in school uniform and Emma assumed she was having a few days off to recover from the news. The duffle-coat she wore was far too big, her shoes were dirty and down at heel and her long dark hair looked uncombed.

'Is he expecting you? If he isn't you could have

lunch with me,' Emma offered, her heart going out to the girl.

Big, blue-grey eyes surveyed her, so like her father's. 'He doesn't know. I left a note at the house in case he went back there.'

'Then there's no reason we can't have a bite to eat together. Shall I leave a note in his surgery as well?'

'He ought to take time off!' Zara burst out resentfully. 'He could have a few days leave, couldn't he?'

'I expect so, but he probably wants to go on working,' Emma said gently. 'It's easier for him to cope if he keeps busy.'

'But what about me? No one cares!' With a sob Zara ran out, and a distraught Emma ran after her.

Zara got as far as the car-park and Emma was nearly up to her when Dr Matthew stopped them both in their tracks. He was just getting out of his car, a thunderous expression on his face. His icy gaze swept over his daughter, whilst ignoring Emma who stood just behind her.

'Get in!' he snapped, holding open the rear door.

Emma waited anxiously, willing the girl to obey him. It would take a very brave or a very foolish person to argue with him in his present mood.

Zara did not move for a few explosive seconds. Then, tossing back her long hair, she did as she was told. Emma let out her pent-up breath. There wasn't going to be a quarrel in public, anyway.

His challenging gaze swept over *her* now, and it took great courage not to run for her life. There was something that needed saying and she might as well be the one to say it, whatever the cost.

'Please don't be hard on her, Doctor. She's . . . she's lost and alone. Life's difficult enough at thirteen.'

In her agitation, she kept turning her wedding-ring around. She still wore it on her third finger. Twisting it around and around gave her comfort.

The doctor's eyes followed the movement, then swung back to her face. 'She isn't thirteen, Mrs Nichols. She's barely twelve. And I know what is best for my own daughter.' The words dripped with ice to match the almost zero temperatures and Emma shivered, suddenly aware of her thin overall.

There was nothing she could do for poor Zara. She had tried and been rebuffed. Perhaps she could do more for Mrs Drummond.

She stood there, despite the biting wind, waiting until the Rover was lost from sight. She lifted her hand to wave to Zara, then lowered it again. The girl was sitting in the back seat, head bowed, and would not see the gesture.

Almost sobbing at the futility of it all, Emma ran back to the warmth of the health centre. Physician, heal thyself, was her last thought before she left for her lunch-break.

Saturday morning it snowed. Emma awoke with a throbbing headache after a virtually sleepless night. She shivered as she peeked out at the weather. Not much snow, not enough to make snowmen, though she saw two boys scraping together enough for a snowball.

She felt like nothing on earth, but maybe it would

be a good day to call on this Mrs Drummond. She saw from the address that she lived in the poorer part of Calbridge. The houses were old there, mostly divided into flats and bed-sitters a bit like her own, but much cheaper.

She could picture it. Miles of lino-covered stairs with squeaking boards and inadequate lavatory facilities. Unheated except by a minute electric fire or an out-of-date oil heater . . .

The more she dwelt on it, the keener she was to see that Mrs Drummond was all right. There was always the danger of hypothermia. Yes, she would go straight after breakfast.

Breakfast was a slice of buttered toast and a cup of black coffee. Sometimes Emma had grapefruit as well, or an apple, but she could not face either this morning.

Dressed in her warmest skirt, hooded anorak and long boots, she ventured out into the morning, to find it not so cold as she'd thought. Even now the snow was thawing and it raised her spirits a bit.

But they plummetted down to her boots when she saw Dr Matthew's sleek blue Rover approaching. He could not, of course, be calling on her. Probably he was going somewhere for the day. She wondered if Zara was in the car, but as he approached from the direction of Calbridge she saw that he was alone.

He stopped as he passed her, then reversed. Emma, face numb, waited for him to come alongside. Perhaps he wanted to talk to her about Zara. Could she have run away?

'Is she all right?' Emma blurted out as he opened the car window.

'Is *who* all right, Mrs Nichols?' His voice was as cold, as distant as ever. He didn't sound upset and Emma blushed. She'd been stupid again. Of course Zara would not run away.

'I . . . I meant your daughter. She was upset yesterday,' Emma said defiantly. One shaggy eyebrow was raised and that hateful smile came to his face.

'It's Zara that I wanted to speak to you about. Are you going anywhere in particular?'

Miserably, Emma shook her head. The last thing she wanted was a lift. 'Just walking. I like fresh air,' she muttered.

'So do I. Let's walk, shall we?'

Aghast, Emma watched him park his car in the small space in front of the house. Having said she was going for a walk, that was what she must do.

Once around the little park should be enough. Why his company should give her a kind of claustrophobia she didn't know. But she did want to hear his views on Zara and a walk would be much better than sitting next to him in the car.

Matthew-phobia! She must remember that. It was a new disease she'd caught and she hoped its duration would be short. Also that it would not turn out to be fatal! The faintest of smiles touched her mouth and the eagle-eyed doctor commented on it.

'Just a passing thought, Doctor,' she said firmly, wondering how he would react if he knew. Then she timidly enquired how Zara was.

'She isn't taking it very well,' he said morosely,

and Emma's lips tightened.

'You make death sound like a dose of medicine! She needs time to grieve. We all do, Doctor.'

'Are you still grieving, Mrs Nichols?'

'Yes, a little. It's only just a year. I feel as . . . as if I've lost part of me,' Emma admitted, surprising herself by telling him, of all people. Now he would make some cutting remark.

But he did not. 'I understand. Time does heal, you know. It isn't just a platitude.'

He was right. Already she was coming out of her depression, starting to care about other people, feeling for them instead of bemoaning the fate which took away her husband.

'Deborah is very good with Zara,' he said suddenly, as they neared the rear entrance of the park.

'Deborah?' she echoed, perplexed.

'Dr More,' he explained. 'She's good with children. But Zara seemed taken with you.'

Emma couldn't imagine the elegant Deborah More being good with children, but could hardly say so. 'I like Zara—what little I've seen of her.'

'She's at a difficult age. You haven't seen the other side of her!' he laughed, glancing down from his great height.

It was good to hear his laughter, and Emma felt her phobia might lessen in time. Then he spoilt it all by adding, 'Since you are so wrapped up in your own selfish grieving, I don't suppose you'll help Zara?'

Emma stopped. Hands on hips, she eyed him, scornfully. 'That was a hateful thing to say! I am not selfish. If I can help Zara then I will,' she finished.

He stood his ground, smiling smugly. He was bare-headed and that little curl was still in its correct place. Even in his khaki ski-jacket and cords he exuded masculinity, charm. He was, of course, as handsome as ever—and as aware of it as ever, Emma decided. She doubted if he had ever felt sorrow, ever cried for a loved one. Not even his sweet daughter could pierce his shell of smug indifference. Doctor he might be, but she doubted if he genuinely cared for anyone except Matthew Scofield.

Her unflattering thoughts must have shown in her expression, for he laughed, a bitter sound this time. 'You really dislike me, don't you?' It was a statement rather than a question, and Emma didn't trouble to reply. What was the point in lying to the man?

'Do you dislike *all* men because yours has gone? Or is it something about me personally, I wonder?' he continued.

Stung, Emma snapped, 'It's purely personal, Dr Matthew. It's you I dislike. You're smug, self-satisfied and totally without feeling!' she flung at him.

He shrugged, then ran his ungloved fingers through his hair. The curl stayed where it was.

Triumphantly, Emma told him what she thought about men who put personal vanity above all else. She didn't need the job and if he was forcing her to leave, so be it. She would give him something to remember her by!

'What personal vanity?' he asked, unruffled as ever. Emma pointed to the curl.

'That curl stays in place no matter what you do! You must sleep with a roller in it!'

It was childish, bickering like that, but once started Emma could not stop. The dam was breached and she had to go on and on, for the emotional torrent came like a flood.

Her voice rose hysterically as he moved nearer. They were alone in the park, with not even a dog in sight, and she thought he meant to hit her.

'Don't touch me!' she cried. 'Keep away! I . . . I hate you!'

His strong arms encircled her and with a final sob she buried her face in his jacket, her head just coming up to his shoulder. His arms tightened and she heard his voice. Not the words, only the soothing sounds.

Strangely comforted, she snuggled closer, only to feel him push her gently away. 'What would my patients think of me, Mrs Nichols?' he chuckled as he released her.

'I don't think there are any patients in the park, Doctor.' She kept her voice light and he would never know the effort it cost her. She'd made a fool of herself, something she always did in his presence.

'That curl is natural,' he said as they strolled companionably back the way they'd come. 'Not wound up in a plastic roller each night, I mean!'

Emma burst out laughing and he joined in. It felt good. And it was to her great surprise that he asked her to Sunday lunch, arranging to pick her up at her home.

She watched him drive away, her thoughts in

turmoil, her errand of mercy to Mrs Drummond half forgotten. Tomorrow she was lunching with the great man at King's House!

It was Saturday lunch-time when Emma finally got to Mrs Drummond's. She didn't care to drive in snowy conditions unless it could be avoided, so took a bus.

The house was old, its window frames rotting away, a general air of decay everywhere, much as she'd expected. The inside smelled—mostly food smells, but Emma preferred not to investigate too closely. Mrs Drummond lived on the second floor and the stairs were steep and not even lino-covered.

She knocked on Mrs Drummond's room door several times without success and when she tried it, the door was locked. Hoping Mrs Drummond wasn't dead in a chair, Emma knocked on the door just down the corridor. Someone might have news of her.

The door inched open and an old man eyed Emma suspiciously. 'What are you selling?' Surprised, Emma couldn't find words for a moment and the door closed again before she could collect her thoughts. This visiting scheme wasn't getting off to a very auspicious start, but she wasn't going to give in yet!

Knocking on the next door produced no results, though she could hear sounds from within. On the floor below she had better luck, and the elderly couple who answered told her that as far as they knew Mrs Drummond was in.

'She never goes out, dear,' the grey-haired

woman put in. The landlord was an absentee one and no one else had a key, so the couple informed her.

Thwarted, Emma stood undecided for a moment. Probably Mrs Drummond was lying down and didn't care to open the door. She would call again tomorrow.

The snow was almost gone on Sunday, so Emma took the car. Again she hammered on Mrs Drummond's door—so loudly this time that the suspicious man in the room next door actually ventured out to inspect her.

'Is Mrs Drummond deaf? The doctor asked me to call on her,' Emma explained.

At mention of the magic word 'doctor' he was eager to help. Emma showed him the note she was to hand to Mrs Drummond to prove that she was from the doctor, and the man, Mr Wathen, banged on the old lady's door himself, calling out to her.

Emma glanced nervously at her watch. She must get back in good time to change. She was wearing slacks and a green cable-knit sweater, something she had once knitted for Tony. He hadn't liked it and it had lain, unworn, in her wardrobe for goodness knows how long. It was too big and she couldn't turn up at King's House looking like a refugee!

Footsteps echoed as someone shuffled to the door. Emma heard the rattle of a chain, then the door opened a fraction.

'Mrs Drummond? I'm Emma Nichols. Dr Matthew asked me to call,' Emma said quickly, afraid the door would close before she could get in.

There was a sniff, then the door was opened wider and Emma saw a tall, black-eyed woman peering at her. She was probably thin, but the voluminous clothes she wore made her appear large and rather forbidding.

'Doctor sent you?' she wheezed, and Emma showed her the note.

Mrs Drummond peered at it then shook her head. 'Haven't got me glasses. Put them down somewhere. Come in.'

Emma turned to thank Mr Wathen but he had disappeared. Feeling rather like Alice entering Wonderland, Emma ventured into the room.

It was big, clean but dreadfully untidy. Books and magazines were scattered everywhere and all available spaces were occupied by tins. On closer inspection they proved to be food, cat food, and various shades of paint.

Mrs Drummond cleared a space for her on the over-stuffed settee where a ginger cat reclined. It eyed Emma balefully.

She sat on the edge of the couch, careful not to disturb the cat, which closed its eyes and went back to sleep.

Because of her host's deafness, conversation proved difficult. It might have been hilarious as Mrs Drummond misheard word after word, but of course it wasn't.

Emma persevered, knowing that the deaf did not receive the sympathy accorded the blind and the crippled. Tony's late mother had become almost totally deaf and many times Emma had heard him shouting at her in the mistaken belief that if he bellowed at her she could miraculously hear him.

It was a difficult conversation but Emma struggled on. Mrs Drummond managed her own shopping sometimes in the summer, so she did get out, after all, even if she didn't venture out in the snow. The local Boy Scouts provided a shopping service and somehow she got by.

When Emma, suddenly conscious of the time, got up to go, Mrs Drummond pressed her down again and insisted she had a cup of tea. It was nearly twelve by the time she managed to escape, promising to return during that week.

Dr Matthew certainly knew what he was doing, suggesting I visit her, Emma mused. Had he purposely made her first assignment a difficult one? Did he believe she would give up so soon? If he thought that, he didn't know Emma Nichols!

Washing and dressing in a rush did nothing for Emma's nerves, and she almost jumped out of her skin when the bell rang. Since Tony's death she had taken little interest in how she looked, deliberately choosing pale colours that blended in with the background. She was drab, and she knew it. She also knew that, with care, her English rose complexion would show up again, that more nourishing food would fill out her thin figure, that brighter clothes would do wonders for her morale.

Perhaps today was a good day to begin. Instead of the beige suit she'd intended wearing, she chose a peacock blue waistcoat suit. She'd had it for years but it was a style that did not date. She teamed it with a frilly white blouse and even went to the trouble of making up her face. Just foundation and blusher, she decided. She hadn't worn lipstick in a long time.

Feeling more like twenty-six again, she snatched up her bag and jacket and hurried down. Matthew Scofield stepped back in surprise at sight of the newly elegant Emma. She smiled shyly and said she was sorry if she'd kept him waiting.

'I've only just got back from your Mrs Drummond!' she confessed.

'Have you now! And what did you think of her?' he enquired mildly.

'I like her, though it was difficult actually getting in to see her. Once in, it was hard to get out!'

Matthew threw back his head and laughed. Then he squeezed her hand. 'I wondered if you would cope! Come on, lunch will be getting cold.'

The pressure of his fingers on hers revived memories that Emma had kept locked up. She wasn't sure if she wanted the surge of emotion that swept over her, and she was glad when he started the car.

Her thoughts in a muddle, she stared down at her slender hands. It had been a long time . . . But she had been invited to the doctor's house solely to see if she could help his daughter, and she would do well to remember that. The drive took no time at all, and Zara was waiting for them on the doorstep of King's House.

Emma felt that the girl was welcoming her home, and she almost held out her arms, only just remembering in time that she was a guest, a mere receptionist, not even a friend. She and the Scofields moved in different worlds.

CHAPTER FOUR

'Hurry up, Daddy. I'm hungry!' Zara wailed.

'That's all you think about,' her father commented, standing aside to let Emma precede him.

She stepped into the big hall, its warmth coming out to meet her. Zara took her jacket and hung it up. For once the girl was tidy, neat in a brown pinafore dress and checked blouse. Her lustrous dark hair shone with cleanliness and health and Emma longed to tell Zara that she was proud of the effort she was making.

Instead, she asked, 'Did you prepare the lunch?'

Zara pulled a face. 'No, not really. Mrs Fillery— that's Daddy's housekeeper—made the pie and I put it in the oven. It's steak and kidney.'

'Very warming,' Emma said appreciatively.

'Very fattening,' another voice commented, and Dr Deborah More appeared in the sitting-room doorway.

Emma felt she did rather well in not letting her smile slip. Not for an instant did her face register anything other than polite surprise that Dr More was also dining at King's House. Only she knew how she felt, the coldness that crept through her body until she froze inside.

Ruth had mentioned Dr More's interest in Matthew so Emma ought not to be surprised. Deborah More greeted her politely but Emma felt hostility emanating from the other woman. Chilly green eyes swept over the suit which Emma had thought so smart. Seen beside the elegant doctor's outfit her own lost its appeal, came a poor second in style.

Dr More also wore a waistcoat suit, but in a rich dark green velvet. The colour made her reddish hair glow. Her lips were red, her face as carefully made up as usual, and as she moved she sent clouds of a heady perfume into the hall.

Emma sniffed. It was a different perfume from the one Dr More used at the centre, and she genuinely liked the scent. She asked what it was as she followed Deborah into the sitting-room, Zara and her father disappearing in what Emma supposed was the direction of the kitchen.

Dr More shrugged. 'It's a French perfume Matthew bought me for my birthday. Too sophisticated for you, Mrs Nichols.' This remark was accompanied by an icy smile and Emma supposed Dr More was no happier than she was at sharing a meal.

The doctor crossed to the open fire and carefully placed another log on it. Emma decided the white blouse she wore was real silk, now that she could see it better. Silk and velvet and a French perfume. So feminine. Deborah More's curves were feminine, too, unlike Emma's too-small bust and tiny waist.

Although younger than the doctor, Emma felt old and dowdy again. A typical harassed housewife trying to look her best for her husband's boss.

'That's a nice little suit you're wearing,'

Deborah said condescendingly, turning suddenly and catching Emma staring.

'Thank you. I was thinking the same thing about yours!' Emma smiled, determined not to join in the bitching. 'I love velvet and silk. And that colour!'

'Mm. I picked it up in Harrods. I thought you wore only grey and brown. Forgive me, but you always seem so . . . well, *restrained* in the health centre,' Deborah said with a slight smile. 'Now you've blossomed out. The contrast is startling!'

Emma's mouth ached from smiling but she was not going to be thrown. 'I hope that's a compliment!' she said lightly, then heard Dr Matthew chuckle.

'I'm sure Deb meant it as one, Mrs Nichols. She's right. That's a nice little outfit.' He walked over to the fire and Deborah More turned to him with a welcoming smile.

Emma, firmly put down, sank on to the brown velvet settee. Her 'nice little outfit' was one she intended never to wear again!

Conversation was strained during pre-lunch drinks but during lunch it was better because Emma could pretend to be concentrating on her food and didn't feel the need to speak much. Zara, too, was subdued. Matthew and Deborah carried on a conversation of their own, but to give him credit Matthew brought Emma and Zara into the conversation from time to time. Emma kept her replies non-committal and brief, sensing the other woman's impatience and keenness to be the centre of attention again.

She could not say she had liked Deborah More

before, but she hadn't realised just how nasty she could be. If Dr More thought Emma was after the same juicy bone and would fight her for it, she could think again! She was welcome to the arrogant Matthew.

After lunch Emma sensed a restlessness in the lady doctor. This was explained when Matthew appeared in car-coat and gloves. Deb was, he told Emma, on her way to her parents for a few days rest and he was taking her. He hoped Emma wouldn't mind amusing herself for an hour or so. Then he would drive her home.

Emma, of course, was delighted, the more so at the sight of Deborah More's sullen face. In any case, it would give her an opportunity to talk to Zara.

Once the others had gone, Emma found her way to the kitchen. Zara rather offhandedly accepted Emma's offer to dry the dishes but refused to be drawn about Celia's accident.

No matter how Emma tried to manipulate the conversation, Zara wasn't taking the bait. Her contribution was monosyllabic and Emma almost gave up in despair. Only concern for this girl, who was not quite a child and certainly not a woman, prevented her from snapping.

'I didn't know Dr More was going to be on leave,' Emma said, giving up the idea of drawing the girl's grief.

'Oh, her! She says I have to call her Aunt Deb. Stupid woman!' Zara said disparagingly, and Emma's eyes opened wide.

'Perhaps she cares for you, Zara. She obviously

wants to be your friend,' Emma said, not believing a word of it.

'*She* wants to be Daddy's wife. That's what *she* wants!' Zara flared, angry eyes turned accusingly on Emma.

'Don't wipe the floor with me then!' Emma tried to inject some humour into the conversation, and to her relief, Zara giggled.

'Sorry. I get all worked up.'

Seizing the opening unwittingly offered, Emma put in gently: 'I'm sure your father wouldn't be looking for another wife just yet. Not so soon after . . .' Deliberately she left the sentence unfinished, and Zara did not disappoint her.

'So soon after Mother's death? And her not buried yet!'

'Does it hurt?' Emma persisted, knowing that if she didn't dig harder she might never get the opportunity again.

Zara hesitated. 'No, not really. I never knew Mother. Not well, anyway. Daddy sent me to boarding-school but I stayed only a couple of terms. Before that they had an au-pair. Sometimes I was left with the housekeeper,' Zara went on, and Emma ached for the lonely child.

'I don't suppose you see much of your father,' she put in gently.

'I do now. Since Mother left the last time we've been closer. She drank a lot,' Zara said candidly, and Emma was better able to build up a picture of the marriage.

Matthew working desperately hard, on call sometimes all weekend or at night, and perhaps not taking the trouble to help his wife with her problem. Not having the time, either, Emma acknowledged. And Zara, left to grow up as best she could in an atmosphere of war, mothered by a succession of servants.

Probably Matthew had been right to ban his wife from the house after a succession of brief reconciliations followed each time by the anguish of parting. Such a family background must have caused the girl harm and it was a wonder she wasn't seriously disturbed. Emma thanked her lucky stars for her own stable background, her polite and homely, if rather dull, parents.

Zara was staring at her, the small pixi-ish face on one side. 'You've been drying that plate for ages. Are you all right?' she enquired, and Emma coloured.

'Sorry. I was lost in thought. Trying to imagine what life must have been like for you. When you were a child, I mean,' she added craftily, knowing that twelve-year-old girls did not consider themselves to be children.

Zara looked pleased. 'Yes, it was hard sometimes. Now I'm a teenager it isn't so bad. Daddy and I get on very well. Mostly,' she added honestly, and Emma smiled.

When Dr Matthew returned they were in Zara's bedroom, a large room which he had allowed her to furnish as she wished. The room reflected her artistic tastes. There were the expected pop posters, plus a stereo record-player, but also a bookcase crammed with books on the theatre and ballet, as well as various handicrafts and painting.

'Daddy says I can have a portable TV when I'm fourteen. Do you think I'm too young now? Daddy says . . .'

She broke off as her father's huge frame filled the doorway. 'Daddy says this and Daddy says that,' he commented, his eyes resting on Emma rather than on his daughter. 'Mrs Nichols will be sick of hearing Daddy's opinions!'

'No, she won't!' Zara said quickly. 'She likes listening to me. Not like *her*!' she went on.

There was a deathly silence and Emma knew Zara had been referring to Dr More. Anxious to ease matters, she rose, slender and graceful, and smiled coolly at her host.

'It's time I went home, Dr Matthew. Zara has entertained me very well. I didn't realise the time.'

Indeed it was nearly four o'clock and Emma wondered why it had taken so long for the short journey. Perhaps they stopped in a quiet byway.

The thought disturbed her, and remained with her during the drive home. Zara accompanied them, she and Emma companionably sharing the back seat.

Of course, she had to be shown over Emma's bed-sitter exclaiming with delight when she saw the rocking-chair.

Dr Matthew smiled wryly as his daughter rocked to and fro. 'That's another item you will be wanting in your room, I suppose?'

Zara nodded enthusiastically, and Emma and Dr Matthew laughed. The laughter hurt Emma, cut her to the quick. It was so much like being part of a family.

Zara was the family she would never have. She supposed that if Matthew married Deborah More they would not provide Zara with a brother or sister. She estimated Deborah to be about the same age as Matthew, so the woman wouldn't want to be burdened with a child. It was perfectly understandable, yet Zara needed brothers and sisters. Someone to care for, help to rear. It was unfair to her.

Momentarily, she closed her eyes, feeling that tears were not far away. To her horror, when she opened them again Matthew was sitting in the rocking-chair—Tony's rocking-chair.

It seemed so natural. He looked right.

Even so, it was wrong of him to sit in her husband's favourite chair. Wrong of her not to mind, as well.

She pictured Tony sitting there, superimposing his face upon Matthew's. The tears spilled over before she could stop them, and she coloured fiercely, turning away from father and daughter. Having only the one room of her own there was nowhere to run to, no place to hide.

Zara started to speak, then Emma heard Matthew's deep voice. His arms went around her and he led her gently towards the settee. She rested her head on the doctor's broad, comforting shoulder, feeling indescribably weary.

'Talk about him if it helps.' He spoke almost in her ear, his breath warming her neck.

She wriggled closer, lost in her memories. 'He was a lot older than me. That rocker—it was his favourite chair. It was just seeing someone else sitting in it that . . . that was what brought on this display of emotion!' She tried to make a joke of it, but her voice cracked. 'I still miss him, but it gets easier.'

'I miss my wife, despite everything,' he said hesitantly, and she gazed up at him, seeing the sensitive, caring man under the hard, arrogant exterior. Their eyes met for a long moment, then Emma glanced away.

She thought his expressive eyes held love but must have been mistaken. It was a moment shared, a moment of deep understanding between two people who had both suffered a loss. Probably they would never be as close again.

Suddenly remembering the child, she looked around for her.

'I told Zara to wait outside. I must go.' In a moment Dr Matthew was all briskness again, the GP who had comforted the bereaved, given his opinion and written out the appropriate prescription.

Feeling foolish because she'd thought for a moment they had shared something wonderful, Emma saw him out, gave the anxious Zara a wan smile, then closed the door firmly. Closed the door on wishful thinking, as well.

As winter progressed to a warm and early spring, Emma gradually settled down at the health centre, finding the duties exacting. As well as acting as receptionist-cum-typist for the doctors, she also helped out at the chiropody clinic, where she met many of Dr Matthew's elderly patients.

Then there was the well-baby clinic where she

helped out for one unforgettable week. There were babies everywhere. Fat ones, thin, scrawny ones, black and brown as well as white. She fell for a set of twins whose young mother was newly married. As like as two peas in a pod, they gazed up at Emma as she cradled them in her arms while the health visitor advised the mother on their care.

Two baby boys. She felt her mother-instinct coming to the fore and was reluctant to return them to their rightful owner. One even made a gurgling, cooing noise at her, and her heart almost broke. If only Tony hadn't been so self-centred she might have had a child to love.

The thought alarmed her. She, who idolised Tony, had actually acknowledged his self-centredness!

Hastily she handed the babies back to the young mother. It was wicked of her and she must not dwell on her childlessness again. It was her fault as much as Tony's probably. If she'd really wanted to, she could have done something about it.

As well as occasionally visiting patients of the practice she had called on Mrs Walker in her small bungalow in Penlow and they had become firm friends. Emma was grateful for the old lady's friendship and was pleased that she had made such a good recovery.

With the doctors, too, Emma was gradually becoming one of the family. Deborah More kept her at a distance, deliberately flaunting her relationship with Dr Matthew in Emma's face. She spoke often of concerts, theatre visits, intimate dinners she'd enjoyed with Matthew. Emma always listened dutifully, putting in a word here, a question there, never betraying the strange hurt she felt at these confessions.

She learned that Deborah More often spent weekends at King's House and Dr More never failed to inform her when such a weekend was coming up, perhaps hoping that it would spoil Emma's own weekend as she visualised them together.

To Emma's shame, it did so. She'd thought she hadn't a jealous bone in her body, but she was now learning otherwise. She could picture them strolling in the huge, untidy garden or sitting down to a meal in the panelled dining-room with Zara. Later on, when Zara was in bed, they danced to records in Matthew's comfortable study. That wasn't simply her imagination, for Deborah told her about it. And she had seen the study on her visit to the house. Seen the record-player, the extensive pile of records.

It was all too clear to Emma that it was only a matter of time before an engagement was announced. Matthew was presumably waiting until a decent interval had elapsed after Celia's death. And since they hadn't been living together, no one, least of all Emma, expected it to be a long interval.

The other doctors were kind, friendly but a little distant. They were busy men, preoccupied by weighty matters. Dr Stephen Dutton was the exception. He often sought Emma out, asked her how she was, listened to her when she had any suggestions to make. And one day in spring, when the tulips were coming into their own, Stephen Dutton waved two concert tickets at her.

Smilingly, she refused. 'I'm sorry, I can't help you out, Doctor. I could use only one, and a couple might be glad of both tickets. Perhaps Ruth Evans?' she suggested, wishing she was part of a couple again.

'They *are* being used by a couple. Us,' he said confidently, causing Emma to open her deep blue eyes wider. 'Do you good. An early dinner, emergencies permitting, then a concert. I shan't take no for an answer,' he said firmly, so Emma meekly agreed to go.

She was astonished as much as pleased. Dr Dutton had always been pleasant to her, shown consideration for her ideas, listened when she spoke about any of his elderly patients she'd visited, but it seemed incredible that he should be interested enough to invite her out.

Why, it must be all of two years since she'd been anywhere. Wining and dining were never Tony's idea of an evening's pleasure and Emma, too, preferred a quiet dinner beside the fire. She had been content before, but now she realised that somewhere she had missed out. She'd become a middle-aged, married woman, trying hard to fit the mould Tony had cast for her.

She *would* go out with Stephen Dutton! It was time she enjoyed herself. The invitation was probably because his regular date couldn't go, but the reason was immaterial. That he had asked her was enough. She was so pleased, she actually beamed at Dr Matthew when he passed her desk a few minutes later.

A startled expression crossed his handsome face, and Emma coloured. 'Happy about something, are we?' he asked acidly.

'You ought to be happy for me, Dr Matthew,' she said evenly. 'You told me I ought to stop grieving, get out and about more. Well, I am!'

She refrained from telling him about Dr Dutton's invitation, feeling sure he would not appreciate private arrangements being made during working hours. But unfortunately, Ruth Evans came bustling up as Matthew moved away and her loud voice must certainly have carried to him as he went into his surgery, leaving the door ajar.

'Fancy young Steve Dutton asking you out!' Ruth trilled, dark eyes dancing.

Emma's heart sank. 'He had two tickets for a concert, Ruth, that was all. I expect he couldn't get rid of them.'

'Oh, no! He bought them special.' Ruth insisted. 'He told me. Had to get up his courage to ask you, he did. I told him you don't bite, though.'

'Thank you,' Emma said dryly. 'I suppose you told him to invite me to dinner, as well?'

Ruth giggled, then Emma saw Dr Matthew's door close quietly. Retribution would follow, that was a certainty. The only question was when.

The meal was excellent the following evening, and Emma could not recall when she'd enjoyed an outing more. Although she still had the appetite of a bird, she managed a prawn cocktail and some chicken Maryland. Stephen Dutton kept up a flow of witty conversation and Emma responded to his warmth like a slender golden flower uncurling its petals in the light of the sun.

She took pains with her appearance, too. Although she wore only the minimum of make-up, her short, corn-gold hair shone with health. She wore a rose-pink knitted dress, the material hugging her figure, and she'd brought out the minute diamond earrings which her parents had given her on her twenty-first birthday.

That birthday seemed years and years ago. For far too long she had felt fifty-six rather than twenty-six and she blossomed under Stephen's admiring gaze. He could not know that each time she looked at him she was seeing the scowling face and stormy blue-grey eyes of another doctor. Try as she might, she could not get Matthew's image out of her mind.

The concert was of Mahler and Strauss, two composers Emma did not particularly care for. Stephen seemed lost in the music, though, and when he reached for her hand during one particularly moving passage she did not demur. Holding hands meant nothing. He was simply a colleague. No more than that.

He drove her home. She hesitated when he stopped the car outside the block of bed-sitters. Should she invite him in for coffee? It seemed churlish not to, yet she lived in one room and it made things awkward.

Thankfully, he seemed not to expect coffee, nor to expect a goodnight kiss, either. He leaned towards her, then merely squeezed her hands before getting out and opening the passenger door for her.

'Goodnight, sweet Emma. Dream of me!' he teased, before driving off into the night.

Reluctantly she turned, wishing he had waited to see her safely indoors.

The evening was cold and dark, with no moon, and she started back in fear as a figure materialised out of the gloom.

CHAPTER FIVE

'YOU CAME straight back then?'

Emma's heart started fluttering again, but not with fear this time. Dr Matthew's deep voice was the most welcome sound in the world at that moment. At any moment, come to think of it!

Breathlessly, she nodded. Realising he couldn't see her, she moved into the light cast by the street-lamp. 'Yes, we left when the concert finished. There wouldn't have been much point in staying!' she added lightly, but there was no answering laughter from the darkness.

She could just see the big doctor's outline, but there was insufficient light to see the expression on his face. It would be disapproving, of course. Sudden resentment flared in her. What right had he to spy on her? Why should it matter to him if they'd lingered on the drive back?

'Were you checking up on me?' Emma put as much ice into her voice as she could. 'If so, I consider it impertinent. I haven't got designs on Dr Dutton, if that is what's bothering you!'

He moved nearer. Now she could see his expression she found it not so much disapproving as worried. Anxiously she put out a hand to comfort him, but snatched it back just in time. 'Zara? Is she all right? Not sick or—or anything?'

His brows met in a dark frown, and Emma

sighed. She'd said the wrong thing again. Indeed, when did she ever say or do the right thing where this arrogant man was concerned?

'Why should you be interested in Zara?' he enquired, his tone irritated. 'She is my daughter, not yours,' he added.

Feeling acutely uncomfortable, Emma murmured, 'Yes, Doctor.' It came easily to an ex-nurse. Never argue with doctors. There was no way one could win. Doctor always knew best, didn't he?

In this case, though, the doctor did not know best. Zara needed a woman to turn to! Emma realised the girl probably confided in Ruth Evans, so she wasn't as badly off as it might seem on the surface, but even so . . .

'Would you have liked a daughter, Mrs Nichols?' he enquired softly, breaking into Emma's train of thought.

'I . . . yes, I would,' she admitted. 'My husband didn't want one, though. Perhaps it was for the best,' she added reflectively. 'I might not have been a good mother. Who knows?' Restlessly she turned to go, hoping he would not expect an invitation to coffee.

'You would make an excellent mother. In my humble opinion,' he added, sounding anything but humble.

Startled, she could only stand and stare. Then he held out his hand and Emma hesitantly took it.

His soft laughter echoed in the night. 'The key, Mrs Nichols! I was about to open the front door and see you safely inside.'

The words 'since your escort didn't bother' hung

unsaid in the air between them as a crimson Emma fumbled in her bag for the key.

Once safely back in her room, Emma flopped down onto the settee, her mind in a whirl, for as soon as Dr Matthew had unlocked the front door, he had departed with a curt, 'Goodnight,' leaving her staring after him in perplexity.

Now she couldn't concentrate, could think of nothing save Matthew Scofield. Why he had come was a puzzle. It could not be that he wanted to see her safely home. He might have expected Stephen Dutton to see her indoors. She could well have invited Stephen up for coffee or a nightcap. And if she *had* asked Stephen up, would Dr Matthew have still lurked in the shrubbery, watching and waiting?

His presence here tonight did not make sense, but Emma was too overwrought to ponder on it. Right now she needed her bed. But tired as she was, it took hours for her to fall asleep. Images of Dr Matthew kept popping into her mind. She finally fell asleep staring into those quizzical blue-grey eyes.

Friday was a red-letter day for Emma as far as visiting the elderly went, for she finally persuaded Mrs Drummond to venture out in the car. Although during the fine weather Mrs Drummond usually went out to get her bits of shopping, she had never been in a car for a joy-ride. Indeed, the hospital car service was her only experience of cars.

Emma had suggested a trip down to Brighton, and the old lady hesitantly agreed. When Emma left a note for Dr Matthew to this effect, he had surprised her by his enthusiasm, suggesting that his daughter might go too. Zara was good with the elderly and Mrs Drummond might prove rather a handful for one person and might distract Emma's attention while she was driving.

He made no mention of the concert and of his concern to see her safely indoors. Stephen Dutton had asked Emma the following morning if she had enjoyed herself and when she thanked him politely and said she had, he suggested they might fix up another concert sometime. Emma had smilingly agreed but tried, at the same time, to show him she wasn't enthusiastic at the idea.

What, she wondered, would he say if she told him Dr Matthew had finished off the evening very nicely for her? Now if *he* were to ask her out, it would be a different matter!

Brighton seemed, on reflection, too far to drive Mrs Drummond. She might become restless. Then there was the problem of having to keep stopping so the old lady could use the lavatory. Emma settled instead upon Little Upwell, which wasn't as far east as Brighton, yet boasted a sheltered bay and a few shops. It was the sea-air that Mrs Drummond was keen on and it would be more pleasant for her in the quiet bay, which was never visited by the large crowds that were attracted to the far greater amenities of Brighton or Eastbourne. Emma's parents lived in Eastbourne and would have welcomed Mrs Drummond, but that was for later, when the old lady grew in confidence.

Dr Matthew rearranged the shifts so that Emma could have the whole of Friday off, working instead

on the Saturday morning. That meant an early
start, Emma thought hopefully, but by the time the
procrastinating Mrs Drummond was ready it was
gone eleven o'clock. And then Zara suggested that,
as they were so late, they might as well wait for her
father, who had the rest of Friday free after his
morning round. Emma stared, aghast at the idea
of driving the formidable Dr Matthew to Little
Upwell.

'I'm not sure we should wait that long,' she said
hesitantly. She didn't want to disappoint the girl
but her father's presence would play havoc with her
concentration!

It simply wasn't on, and a disgruntled Zara
finally saw the sense of getting away as soon as
possible. Now the old lady was ready she was keen
to be away, and sat fidgeting on the edge of the
over-stuffed settee, large handbag and umbrella
clutched firmly to her chest.

The ginger cat was alert and watchful, and Mrs
Drummond was heard to murmur that she would
be back in good time for her darling's dinner. That
clinched it. Giving the animal a wary pat, Emma
shepherded Zara and Mrs Drummond out of the
room and down the steep stairs. She'd been afraid
Mrs Drummond would insist on taking the cat with
her, but fortunately this didn't occur to her until
they arrived in Little Upwell, when she remarked
how much Timmo would have enjoyed a change of
scenery.

'I'm sure he's happier at home,' Zara told her
soothingly. 'Cats don't like change.'

Emma smiled. Her two passengers, so far removed in age, were getting on extremely well. That was often the case. Young people seemed to have an affinity for the old and were often very good with them.

She knew from the records that Mrs Drummond wasn't that old, only in her early seventies.

The schools were still closed for the Easter holidays so the town was more crowded than Emma would have liked, but Mrs Drummond did not appear to mind. Eagerly she went into shop after shop, turning over the neatly stacked merchandise, plucking at a skirt here, a sweater there.

Emma followed Mrs Drummond at a distance, calmly keeping an eye on her. The last thing she wanted was for her to absent-mindedly forget to pay for something.

Once, when she was a student, Emma had placed two birthday cards in her wire basket. Deep in conversation with a nursing colleague she had walked out of the big department store complete with the cards and wire basket! She had gone only a few yards before glancing down in horror and rushing back to the store to pay for the cards, but she'd never forget that embarrassing incident and had sympathy with those who found themselves in a similar predicament.

Remembering that incident, now, she was especially watchful. Mrs Drummond was a collector, principally of paint. Tins of every conceivable colour littered her bed-sitter but she had a special liking for red, and when she headed towards a do-it-yourself shop, Emma began to wonder how many cans could comfortably be filled into the car.

But to her relief, Mrs Drummond bought only one tin of pillar-box red, non-drip gloss, and although she glanced longingly at all the paint in the shop, she appeared content with her purchase.

What amazed Emma most was the thick wad of bank notes that Mrs Drummond pulled from her bag when she came to pay. And then there was the silver! Zara gasped outright as Mrs Drummond emptied the contents of her large pockets onto the check-out counter. She must have had several pounds worth of small coins.

Emma and the assistant exchanged amused glances, but Emma knew that it wasn't really funny. Already, curious glances were being cast at them and interested stares were estimating the amount of cash that lay on the counter. It would be all too easy for someone unscrupulous to take a few notes. Hastily Emma put Mrs Drummond's money back into the handbag and shepherded the protesting woman out of the shop.

'I hadn't finished!' Her loud voice drew the attention of several passers-by and, to her horror, Emma saw a policeman heading purposefully towards them.

'I just didn't want you to leave your money lying around,' Emma said, harassed. 'Someone might steal it,' she pointed out clearly, but apparently not loudly enough, for the old lady cupped her fingers around the back of her ear and leaned forward to catch the words.

Face flushed, Emma repeated her words, a giggling Zara doing nothing to help the situation. Mrs Drummond scowled when she caught the gist of

Emma's remarks, then the young policeman loomed over them.

He seemed younger even than Emma and was not the fatherly, reassuring type of policeman she liked to see.

'Everything all right, Miss?' he asked carefully, keen brown eyes on Emma's embarrassed face.

She nodded, then stammered out that she was a doctor's receptionist taking one of the patients out for the day. Mrs Drummond, meanwhile, stood silently, evidently unable to catch the words. Then, to Emma's horror, she held out her handbag.

'Look! She's been trying to collect my money!'

Zara, a quick-witted girl, explained the situation and fortunately the constable was satisfied. He walked along with them for a few minutes. Mrs Drummond apparently found his presence reassuring.

Dr Matthew Scofield did not. His grim face told its own story as they met him on the road to the sea front. Zara ran to him, but his accusing gaze was upon Emma, the patient and the policeman.

Emma smiled, but Matthew's disapproving expression did not soften.

'It's all right, Doctor. This nice young policeman was just escorting us,' she babbled, and those heavy-lidded eyes rested upon the constable, whom he dwarfed.

Breathlessly, Zara explained to her father what had happened, with Emma contributing a word here and there. The officer had by now continued on his beat.

'You like attracting attention, Mrs Nichols,' the

doctor announced, making the words sound like a death sentence, and Emma winced.

His words hurt her. It was silly, she knew, but they did. She so wanted him to think well of her, be pleased with Mrs Drummond's progress, but everything she did was wrong.

Even as the thought crossed her mind, his words hit her. 'I expect you'll be giving up visiting the elderly now.'

It was a statement and angrily Emma turned on him, eyes flashing blue fire. 'I will not! You seem to think I give everything up at the first hurdle!'

Zara gazed with interest at her father and his receptionist, and Mrs Drummond cupped her hand around her ear again, the better to hear. Red-faced, Emma took Mrs Drummond's arm and walked ahead of the arrogant, fault-finding doctor. She hated the man! He was hateful, loathsome, chauvinistic . . . She couldn't think of any more words to describe him, but more came to her in the car going back. How about stuffy, arrogant, over-bearing, proud. That would do for the time being, she decided as she headed for home. Dr Matthew followed in his own car.

By and large the day hadn't been such a terrible disaster. Apart from that one episode in the shop, she and Mrs Drummond had got on very well. And the elderly lady's delight at seeing the calm, sunlit sea more than made up for Emma's embarrassment earlier.

Mrs Drummond and Zara had strolled along the promenade, with Emma herself walking a few paces behind. Dr Matthew did not, it seemed, want to join their party, for he had jumped down to the shingle beach and strode along several feet below them.

Now and then Emma had surreptitiously glanced down. Once, her startled gaze met his, but he hadn't returned her shy smile.

When they had seen Mrs Drummond safely indoors, Emma stayed to give the woman her tea and Dr Matthew took his daughter home. He was anxious to leave them and kept glancing at his watch. A date with Deborah More, perhaps?

The idea hurt, and that night Emma tried desperately to analyse her feelings for the man.

She didn't like him, so why should she care when he took out the attractive Dr More? It wasn't any of her business. Dr Matthew's private life was his own. If he chose to relax in the company of another doctor, good luck to him.

It must be that she was jealous because she wasn't one of a pair any longer. Although Tony had never been one for evening entertainment, at least he'd taken her out occasionally. If there was some special play or show she had wanted to see then Tony had accompanied her. Reluctantly, certainly, but without grumbling.

Now she was beginning to realise what life was like for single women who were past the first flush of youth for, although only twenty-six, she felt life was finished. She was a spare wheel, of use only if one of the other wheels was faulty.

It was her destiny to be pushed farther and farther back on the shelf, with maybe a yearly dusting, as if she were an ornament! Well, she'd been dusted for this year. Dr Dutton had wined and dined her, so with that she must be content.

That she might need something more, a loving gesture, the arms of a man, she refused to accept. She must be content with whatever came her way. And if Matthew and Deborah were to become engaged she must try to be pleased for them, not scowl out of jealous spite because she was an only one, a has-been.

She *must* be pleased. She *would* be pleased, no matter what it cost. After all, she cared nothing for the man . . .

Life went on much as before, but Emma was aware that her feelings towards Dr Matthew had changed.

Of course, she disliked him still. That much had *not* changed. Yet whenever she was near to him she felt more alive, more of a woman. She could not account for the transformation. Certainly his attitude towards her remained the same—coolness bordering on coldness was the order of the day.

He seemed surprised she still continued with her visits to Mrs Drummond and others on the list he had given her. If it was just a routine visit and there was no change in the patient, Emma did not trouble him. Only if any patient appeared unable to manage, or in need of help, did she report back to him.

Nevertheless, she kept a list of patients visited and every time she called on one she noted it down in her small, neat handwriting with dates and times. This notebook was kept in Dr Partington's room and Emma made sure that the health visitor and Dr

Matthew knew of its existence, just in case. But she was surprised to find Dr Matthew idly flicking through it one morning when she went to fetch some notes from Dr Partington's surgery.

Uncertainty darkened her eyes as she met the cool, candid gaze of Dr Matthew. Was there something wrong with one of her ladies? she wondered. More likely there was some fault in the notes. Dr Matthew was still as quick as ever to point out her faults, apparently deriving great pleasure from so doing.

He was so hateful to her that she wondered why she looked forward to their brief meetings. And yet she did, very much. Often she found herself counting the hours until his rounds were over and he was due back at the health centre.

She worried, too, if he came in late for surgery— a sign that he had been called out during the night and lost some of his precious sleep. It must be her thwarted mother-instinct, she supposed, as she waited, wanly, for his comments.

'You saw Mrs Sayers yesterday?' he queried, and Emma frowned.

'Yes. I visited three old ladies yesterday. Two of them lived . . . No, Mrs Sayers lives alone. I went there first,' she recalled. 'She's a little pink and white woman with permed hair. Rather a pet,' she smiled, but the blue-grey eyes were accusing.

'She died early this morning. Why didn't you tell me she was failing?' he asked, his tone mild but still accusing.

Emma opened her mouth to defend herself, but he didn't let her even start a sentence. He closed the heavy notebook with a snap, then brushed past her, closing the door behind him.

Stunned and shocked, Emma sank down on to Dr Partington's comfortable swivel chair. She clutched the desk for support. Mrs Sayers had died alone, and Dr Matthew believed her responsible!

Of course she wasn't, she assured herself. Mrs Sayers, if she *was* failing, had showed no signs of it. Although eighty-one, she was a sprightly little woman, all bustle and business as Emma's mother would have put it.

She couldn't be dead. She couldn't! She enjoyed life far more than Emma herself.

Emma was still there, staring into space, when Dr Matthew returned . . .

CHAPTER SIX

WEARILY, Emma raised her head. By now she was coldly angry. He was going to blame her for a death she could not have prevented even if she had been there at the time. It wasn't fair, but she was beyond caring.

She rose and picked up her notebook from the top of the desk and put it away neatly in its place. All the time she could feel Matthew's eyes upon her but she refused to meet his condemning gaze. Let him think what he wanted. She knew she was blameless and his opinion no longer mattered. She would continue her work to the best of her ability. She would not give him the satisfaction of seeing her throw in the towel.

'Emma.'

So softly did he speak that Emma wasn't sure she'd heard him. It was obviously her mistake because he'd never called her anything other than 'Mrs Nichols'.

'Emma, I'm sorry.'

This time she knew she wasn't mistaken. Her surprised gaze met his. The big doctor was leaning against the closed door, arms folded defensively, eyes expressionless.

'I had no right to accuse you. There was nothing you could do for the woman,' he admitted.

Emma floundered, not knowing how to cope

with this unexpected side of his nature. She was thrown completely, just when she had convinced herself how much she disliked the man!

'It's all right,' she managed at last, realising how much that apology must have cost him.

'I should not have spoken as I did,' he said gruffly, and Emma smiled tentatively.

How nice it would be to be friends with this man, she thought wistfully. The burden of his dislike weighed heavily upon her at times, making her clumsy, causing her to commit errors she would not otherwise have made.

'If only we could be friends!' she burst out, surprising herself.

A startled expression crossed Matthew's handsome face, then he smiled a trifle ruefully. 'I doubt that's possible, Mrs Nichols.'

Rebuffed, Emma flushed and hot tears pricked her eyelids.

'Oh, God! I didn't mean to say that!' Suddenly he was by her side, his hands gripping her upper arms, hurting her.

He gave her a little shake. 'I always say the wrong thing, don't I?' he murmured. And then an amazed Emma found herself being thoroughly kissed.

His hands slid down her arms, then encircled her waist, holding her pressed closely to the length of his body.

She felt the erratic beat of his heart as they stood entwined. Or it could have been her own heart that pounded away, doing aerial acrobatics within her breast.

His kiss was long and hungry, demanding and

receiving from Emma all she had to give. Love was never like this! she remembered thinking—and then abruptly he pushed her away, his eyes mirroring her own shock. Before she could make light of the incident, assure him she understood, he was gone, the door slamming noisily behind him.

Emma, stunned and shaken, slid down into Dr Partington's chair. She was incapable of coherent thought, incapable of movement.

It's shock, she assured herself. Sit with your head lower than your heart and fresh, oxygenated blood will get to your poor brain.

Dr Matthew must be very hard up if he needed to kiss me, she reflected, when she finally got up, ran shaking fingers through her hair, then left the office. He had the available and obviously willing Deborah More. Surely he did not need the mousy Mrs Emma Nichols as well?

Dr Matthew had, apparently, put the incident from his mind the moment it was over, for he greeted Emma in his usual aloof manner the next time they met.

He was throwing a birthday party for his daughter, he told her, and Zara had asked if she might invite Emma.

'Birthday party?' Emma echoed, recalling that a few months before he'd told her Zara was barely twelve.

He nodded. 'More an un-birthday party, really. It's for her twelfth. She didn't have a party then, so I've promised her one now.'

The idea of the big, surly doctor being badgered into providing a party a struck Emma's funny-bone and she laughed. Watchful blue-grey eyes rested upon her, then he smiled slightly.

'She keeps wheedling concessions out of me,' he admitted. 'Says she wants to visit you, sometimes, and sit in your rocking-chair,' he added, his words catching Emma off-balance.

'Does she? I . . . I'm glad. I enjoy her company. Can she? Visit me, I mean?'

'If you're sure she won't be a nuisance I should be pleased,' he said formally, and Emma couldn't tell by his tone of voice whether he actually approved.

She had to decline the invitation to the party, though, on grounds of a previous engagement, and Dr Matthew's brows were raised. He made no comment, however, and Emma did not offer the information that her previous engagement was auxiliary nursing at the local hospital, something she had just started.

Not wanting to ask him for a reference, she had asked Dr Partington instead, and as far as she was aware no one else knew about the extra work. It was satisfying and fired her enthusiasm anew to return to 'proper' nursing, resume her training or perhaps train as an SEN instead. She had no burning ambition to become a ward sister or nursing officer. Just as long as she could do bedside nursing she would be content.

Soon after that, Zara's visits began, brief ones at first and irregular but gradually becoming more frequent. Usually she stayed for a snack meal, and Emma enjoyed planning little treats for her.

Buck rarebit was something Zara had never tried before, and Emma prepared her chilli con carne for supper one day. Zara enjoyed it and asked for the recipe so that she could try it out on her father. Pleased that Dr Matthew would be eating one of her own favourite meals, Emma wrote out the instructions.

In the meantime, she continued with her work at the health centre. Even in the warmer months of the year it was tremendously busy at the centre. There were ante-natal, child health, family planning and school health clinics each week, plus sessions especially for the elderly. Chiropody clinics were held twice weekly and were always crowded.

In addition, Dr Matthew and Dr Partington ran a club for the old folk with the help of the health visitor and social worker, and Emma gladly volunteered to help there, even though her other duties were onerous. Zara was interested and joined her one afternoon to help run a tea-party for the elderly patients.

Although strickly speaking it was nothing to do with Dr More, she, too, was there, directing operations. Indeed, since she'd seen the amount of work Emma was doing for Dr Matthew's patients she had been much in evidence.

Dr Matthew himself was holding his ante-natal clinic but would pop in later. Dr Partington was there together with several of the health centre staff, but it was Deborah More who was obviously in charge, her sharp green eyes resting upon Emma from time to time. Emma felt uncomfortable, just as she had months ago, when lunching at King's House.

There was no question of trying to look smart today. She had discarded her pink overall but wore a sensible and dowdy grey fleck dress. But because it was a party she had clipped her gold and ruby brooch to the collar, and several of the ladies complimented her on it.

Their eldest patient, a lady of ninety-six, was examining it when Emma sensed Dr More's heavy perfume and knew she had drawn close. Emma tensed, waiting for some snide remark. The patient, Miss Tuttle, was quite deaf so Dr More would feel safe in passing some seemingly innocent yet barbed comment on Emma's appearance. It had become a regular occurrence.

But this time she had an eavesdropper, and Zara, who heard Dr More's disparaging remark about 'tinsel jewellery', flounced off pointedly, with an unmistakable glare at the lady doctor. Secretly pleased, but trying not to show it, Emma pretended she hadn't noticed either of them, and escorted Miss Tuttle towards a comfy seat.

Later, when Matthew appeared, Emma saw Deborah whispering in his ear, gesturing with one slim hand towards Zara, who was helping an old man into his overcoat. Emma bit her lip, suddenly afraid for Zara. Her response to Dr More was rude, even though it was justified, and Deborah was the intended second wife of Zara's father. One day, soon perhaps, she would become Zara's step-mother and could then take out her ire on the girl.

Nothing was said that day but next morning,

directly surgery was over, Dr Matthew called Emma into his office and savagely tongue-lashed her.

His daughter, he announced, was becoming unmanageable, rude and sharp-tongued. She had behaved disgracefully to poor Deborah the previous afternoon, and had apparently been egged on by Emma. 'You are an unfortunate influence on my daughter, Mrs Nichols!' he said forcefully, almost breathing fire.

It was ludicrous! She was a grown woman and Dr Matthew had no business speaking to her as though she were some naughty and dim-witted child. When she told him so he scowled, surprised perhaps that Emma should dare to take him to task.

He reddened, and Emma felt sorry for him, despite his harsh and unjust words to her. Deborah More had him just where she wanted him and he couldn't see how malicous the woman was being.

'Deborah feels she is fitter company for Zara than an in . . . than a grieving widow.' Hastily he changed the sentence, but Emma pounced.

'Was *inadequate* the word you were seeking, Doctor?' she asked smoothly.

Obviously discomfited, he nodded. 'I'm sorry, Mrs Nichols, but I don't think Zara should spend so much time with you.'

'Do *you* consider me inadequte? An unfit companion for your daughter?' Emma challenged, fists clenched by her sides.

'I have to decide what's best for my daughter!' he snapped. 'Deborah and I are good friends and I can't let Zara insult her.'

'Not if Dr More is going to be Zara's stepmother. I can quite see your difficulty,' Emma said acidly.

A faint smile crossed his face. 'Is Deb going to be Zara's stepmother? No one told me.'

'It's a forgone conclusion.' Emma's tone was crisp. 'Dr More evidently believes it to be only a matter of time. Please excuse me.' She walked with dignity to the surgery door.

Ruth Evans eyed her as she came out. 'Not causing trouble is she? That Deborah More, I mean. She doesn't like you.'

'So I gathered,' Emma said quietly, then began tidying the magazines ready for the evening surgery. That done, and still burning with indignation, she hurried upstairs to the child guidance clinic. There had been a session that morning and because the secretary was away Emma had been asked to type the reports.

The child psychiatrist, a tall, balding and vague-looking man was still there, and Emma spent a few moments chatting with him before she settled down to type his letters. A sound made her glance up as she struggled to read the educational psychologist's writing a little later.

Zara stood there, her face grimy and tear-stained. Without a word, Emma rose and held out her arms and the tall, lanky girl ran to her, burying her face in Emma's hair.

Sobs shook her frame and Emma let her cry. Once the grief was past Zara would feel better, no matter how great the trouble that had caused it. Unfortunately, Dr More was passing on her way out to visit patients, and her full lips tightened at

the scene. Her green eyes met Emma's accusingly.
Then she was gone, and a worried Emma shook the
girl gently.

'Zara. What is it? Do you want to talk about it?'

Surely Dr More hadn't been on at her? No, she
would leave that to Matthew. She would not want
to get involved with tiresome teenage emotions.

'I've run away from school!' Zara announced
dramatically, and Emma's heart sank.

Matthew had enough troubles without Zara
adding to them, she mused, surprising herself by
worrying about his well-being. It was Zara for
whom she ought to feel concern.

Zara, she discovered, had fallen foul of a new
teacher. Whenever the teacher and the wilful, high-
spirited girl clashed, poor Zara was reported to the
head, who was now threatening to inform Dr
Matthew.

'He'll sigh and rub the back of his neck,' Zara
told her. 'Then he'll pace up and down, muttering
to himself. Next comes the reproachful look, that
hurt expression he gets when I've done wrong,' she
went on soulfully, and Emma almost laughed, despite the seriousness of the situation. The girl's
description of her father was a graphic one.

Emma could see him pacing the study, dark hair
tousled, though that immaculate little curl would
be in its place. His expressive blue-grey eyes would
be brooding, intense, full of hurt that his only child
should cause him such pain.

Quickly Emma shut out the scene she had
pictured. It was no business of hers. Serve him right
for being an inadequate parent.

Comforting the girl was comparatively easy; persuading her to return to school was impossible. Zara was adamant. She turned her big eyes upon Emma with that troddon-on puppy expression Emma knew so well—for Dr Matthew had it down to a fine art, too!

She knew she must tell him, perhaps help him see his daughter's side of the affair. He wouldn't want Zara to end up in the child guidance clinic. Of course Zara was far from needing the help the clinic could provide, but Dr Matthew had a problem on his hands nevertheless.

It was difficult to know what to do. Zara was too old to be smacked like a child, but reasoning with her often didn't work. Her age was a particularly traumatic and emotional one. If she received the correct guidance and firm handling now, she might turn out to be a sweet-natured, if occasionally rebellious teenager. But given Dr Matthew's temper and well-intentioned but sometimes unwise laying down of the law to his daughter, Zara might turn into a teenage drop-out with no prospects, no hope, no love for anyone.

That Matthew loved his wilful daughter Emma did not doubt for a moment. He did not show it enough, and an uncertain, anxious Zara did not always know where she stood.

Emma's heart ached for the girl. If only she had the right to take Dr Matthew to task, discuss the problem with him, plan together with him how Zara might be helped. If anyone could help him to understand his daughter it should be Deborah More.

Emma's indecision showed in her face once Zara had wandered disconsolately away, having promised to return at lunch-time for another talk. Despite Emma's pleas, she refused to wait at the centre and had presumably gone for a cup of coffee somewhere.

Cash didn't seem to be a problem for her. She seemed well-supplied with pocket-money. So well-supplied that she had sufficient to live on when she ran away.

This startling news came to Emma's ears when a fierce Dr Matthew hurled himself through the health centre door late that afternoon. Eyes blazing, he glared down at his receptionist, who half rose, a nameless fear tugging at her insides.

'Zara!' the big doctor ground out, and Emma sat down again wearily.

'What has she done now?' she asked, blue eyes anxious and very appealing as they rested upon him.

He stifled a sigh. 'She's run away, Mrs Nichols, and Deborah says you know where she has gone!'

Emma shot up, as angry as the doctor now. 'No, I do *not* know where she is! The child could be anywhere, wandering lost and alone. Penniless,' she went on, her imagination picturing nameless horrors for the attractive girl.

'She isn't penniless. She has adequate pocket-money,' he said more gently.

He sank down onto the hard chair in front of Emma's small desk.

'Oh, Dr Matthew! I wish I could help,' she breathed, realising the stupidity of her words.

Coping daily with the lives of others, how can they begin to deal with emotions such as love?

Take four books FREE

Also FREE — a fashionable canvas bag

Four specially selected
Doctor Nurse Romances – FREE

In the high-pressure life of a busy hospital, people find themselves unexpectedly drawn together. Perhaps it's the daily tragedies and ordeals of working with the weak and helpless, perhaps it's the shared satisfaction of a difficult job well done — whatever the causes, people find themselves involved not only with their work....but with each other.

Send today for your Four Free Books, and reserve a Reader Service Subscription for eight brand new Doctor Nurse Romances every two months, delivered to your door postage and packing free. And you can enjoy many other advantages:

 No commitment — you receive books for only as long as you want.

 Free newsletter — keeps you up-to-date with new books and book bargains.

 Helpful friendly service from the girls at Mills & Boon. You can ring us anytime on 01-684 2141.

FREE BAG **Our exclusive white canvas tote bag with the Mills & Boon symbol — yours FREE — whatever you decide!**

A subscription to Doctor Nurse Romances costs just £8.00 every two months, but send no money now — these four books are yours to keep — **FREE.** You have nothing to lose — fill in the coupon today.

Postage will be paid by Mills & Boon Limited

Do not affix postage stamps if posted in Gt. Britain, Channel Islands or N. Ireland.

BUSINESS REPLY SERVICE
Licence No. CN 81

Mills & Boon Reader Service,
PO Box 236, Thornton Road,
CROYDON, Surrey CR9 9EL.

Naturally she wished she could help, but it was useless to say so.

'She ran away from school this morning,' she said quietly, and he looked at her, exhausted now, not angry. In his eyes Emma recognised mute appeal.

It was too much, and she began to cry. With tears streaming down her face, she realised that Matthew had come around the desk. Then he wrapped her in his arms and they held each other tightly, their grief uniting them.

CHAPTER SEVEN

HASTILY they broke apart as footsteps echoed in the corridor. It was Dr Matthew who drew back first, and a discomfited Emma sat back in her chair, face flushed, heart pounding.

She had behaved foolishly and Dr Matthew would despise her for her display of emotion. Yet to cling to him seemed so right in their moment of need.

'Wh . . . where do you think Zara might be?' she whispered, just as Ruth Evans came into view, her usually merry eyes sad and subdued.

He shrugged. 'Celia had no close relatives except for her father and he's abroad now. My father lives in Southampton but she hasn't gone there. What about you?' he asked, as if the idea had suddenly struck him.

'Me? What about me?' Emma floundered.

'Haven't you some relatives? Zara spoke of your parents in Eastbourne.'

'So she might have done, but she has never met them,' Emma emphasised, but the expression in Dr Matthew's eyes was unfriendly now. Gone was the camaraderie of a moment ago.

'Are you sure she isn't there?' he persisted.

'Why on earth should she visit *my* parents when your father is so much nearer? It doesn't make sense,' Emma pointed out, well aware that Deborah More was the cause of Matthew suspecting her.

'I'm sorry,' he said softly, his brooding gaze on her. Then he turned to Ruth, who shook her head wearily.

'No news from any of her school-friends, Doctor. I've asked my Mandy to keep her eyes and ears open. She can't be far, love.' The motherly Ruth put a comforting hand on the doctor's arm and he patted it absently.

'I've more visits to make after surgery. I can't spare the time to search for her. The patients come first.'

This remark was addressed more to Emma than to Ruth, as though he was apologising for not being out scouring the countryside for his daughter.

Emma understood that. With him the patients must always come first, even though he was consumed with personal grief. He would not let his patients down. She was proud of him, admired his dedication, but that same steadfast dedication to duty had helped break up his marriage and now was estranging him from his daughter.

Dr Matthew and Ruth moved away, and a disorientated Emma set about finishing the report she was typing. But then she decided to phone her parents, just in case.

Zara had never seen them but Emma spoke of them often, and the girl had more than once said wistfully that she wished she had a grandmother.

There was no reply from her parents' number, even though Emma let it ring for a long time. They might be out, enjoying a day in the country perhaps.

She left a note for Dr Matthew assuring him that she'd tried to contact her parents without success. Zara did not, in any case, know exactly where they lived.

She might have gone to London, seeking her fortune among the streets paved with gold.

Fear clutched at Emma's heart as she dwelt unwillingly on the idea that evening when she went on her voluntary duty at the hospital. For a while she'd considered either staying at home or hanging around the health centre in case there was word of Zara, but her strong sense of duty prevailed.

Matthew was right. The patients came first and the hospital would expect her to be there. It would, in any case, be better for her to keep busy rather than dwell on the problem.

She finished at nine-thirty. Her duties at the hospital were simple ones, the cleaning of dentures, helping change incontinent patients, giving out evening drinks and so on. Yet she was happy even performing such tasks.

She had tentatively asked about completing her training and the principal tutor was encouraging. It would be good to train in that area. But it meant leaving the health centre, leaving the arrogant, fault-finding but charismatic Dr Matthew.

She drove back slowly, half inclined to call in at King's House but the thought that Deborah More might be there deterred her. She would telephone instead.

There was no telephone in the old house but

there was a telephone-box on the corner and Emma stopped the car, rehearsing in her mind the conversation she would have with Dr Matthew. What could she say? Ought she to ring him at all? He would want to keep the line clear in case someone phoned him with news of his daughter. Finally she decided she would telephone but make it brief and to the point.

Dr Matthew himself answered, his tone betraying no emotion as he spoke.

'So! You're back in circulation, Mrs Nichols.'

'Yes, yes I am. I've been out.' For some reason she didn't tell him about her work at the hospital.

'I went to your home but couldn't get a reply,' the calm, unhurried voice went on, and Emma's eyebrows shot up in surprise. 'For a moment I thought that you—'

He broke off suddenly and she heard his chilly laugh. 'Never mind what I thought. Zara is back home.'

'Thank God!' Emma burst out. 'Where was she? Is she all right? Not . . . not harmed or anything?'

'No, she's fine. You *will* be surprised to learn where she was.' There was no mistaking the ice in his deep voice and Emma went cold.

'Where did you find her?' She kept her voice calm, only faintly interested. She would be blamed wherever the girl had been.

'In Eastbourne, Mrs Nichols. She went to visit her adopted grandparents.'

'What?'

'*Your* parents, Mrs Nichols. Now isn't that strange?'

'It's unbelievable!' Emma said hotly. She'd had enough of this cat-and-mouse game. 'She didn't know their address—or their surname, come to that!'

'Someone must have told her,' Dr Matthew accused, and Emma choked back the words of denial.

'I suggest you ask her how she found out my parents' address,' she said stonily, then replaced the receiver before she said something she might later regret.

Zara was safe and well. That was what mattered. No doubt Deborah More would see that the blame rested squarely upon Emma, but that was a minor irritation.

It was too late to telephone her parents. They were an early to bed, early to rise couple, often up at crack of dawn. Tomorrow would suffice. For tonight all Emma wanted was sleep. She was unutterably weary, drained.

Tomorrow would be a better day, she assured herself. It could hardly be worse.

The following morning the health centre was so busy she hardly saw anything of Dr Matthew, which was a good thing. The waiting area was packed, probably because there was an epidemic of a nasty but short-lived flu-type virus. The weather had turned colder again and wetter, which didn't help.

Dr Dutton phoned to say he was too weak to come in, so his appointments were shared between the others. Dr Raye looked poorly but he struggled on somehow, his only concession to his illness being that he let the others do his rounds after surgery. Through it all, Emma was kept busy dashing back and forth with lists of names, cancelling an appointment here, transferring a patient there.

Old Mr Sims came hobbling in just as Emma thought they had finished for the morning. Dr Matthew took surgery until ten but it was generally eleven or so before he finished. He would not, however, accept patients who arrived after ten as otherwise the list could have gone on until lunchtime. The other doctors made similar provisos, but Emma knew Matthew would want to see Mr Sims even though it was after ten-thirty before he arrived.

He was a terminal cancer patient of about eighty and somehow he managed to keep going. He had a home help but otherwise managed alone.

Smiling resignedly, Emma added his name to Dr Matthew's list. The doctor had only two more patients to see and the waiting room was rapidly clearing. Dr Partington finished and buzzed for Emma to take some dictation as she hurried back to her station with Mr Sims' record card.

She ran her fingers distractedly through her short hair, causing it to stand on end, and it was in the midst of all this that Dr More beckoned to her from the corridor. Tight-lipped, Emma hurried out to her, Mr Sims' card clutched to her chest.

Her green eyes narrowed, Deborah More almost snatched the card. 'Matthew doesn't see patients if they arrive after ten! Surely you know that by now?'

She tapped her foot impatiently, a habit Emma found irritating at any time. At that moment it was too much, and she snapped at the doctor, telling her that Dr Matthew *always* saw Mr Sims, whatever the time of day.

Taken aback, Dr More dropped the card and an angry Emma posted it through Dr Matthew's letter-box, then helped Mr Sims to a seat outside the surgery, where there was a vacant chair.

Eyes blazing, Dr More stalked off. A harassed Emma collected her notebook and flew upstairs to Dr Partington's surgery, an apology trembling on her lips for her lateness.

He was cross, but not because she'd kept him waiting. Reproachful grey eyes watched her uncertain progress.

'You ought not to interfere, Emma,' he said sternly. 'Zara is Matthew and Deborah's concern, you know.'

Weakly, Emma sank onto the chair. 'I don't want to discuss it, Dr Partington. Have you many letters?'

It was the old doctor's turn to be taken aback. The mild-mannered, mousy Emma Nichols almost snapping at him was a new departure. In her turn Emma felt guilty.

Of all the doctors, she liked Dr Partington the most. Much more than Dr Matthew, she told herself silently, as she bent her head and concentrated on the few letters and notes he dictated.

She had no reason to see Matthew until after lunch. She finished at one, then went home for a short break before the afternoon session, which was a family planning clinic.

Dr Matthew met her in the health centre carpark when she returned. His face was drawn, his eyes tired and there was a dejected slump to his shoulders.

'How is Zara?' Emma asked politely.

His lips tightened, then he shrugged. 'Still determined to run away from home at the first opportunity,' he admitted bleakly.

'I'm sure she won't,' Emma reassured him. 'She has a good home. Why did she go to my parents? I rang them at lunch-time and they couldn't understand it.'

There was a pause. 'It appears I owe you an apology, Mrs Nichols. Zara told me she saw a letter from your mother lying around and took the address from that.'

'I wonder why she chose my parents? The obvious haven for her would be your father, surely?'

He gave her a speculative look. 'One would have thought so. Apparently she regards you as her surrogate mother. Therefore your parents are her grandparents. Logical reasoning, I suppose.'

Secretly pleased, Emma murmured that she was sorry Zara considered her a mother-substitute.

'So am I, Mrs Nichols. So am I!' he almost snarled, then strode into the health centre, leaving a saddened Emma to follow.

It was hardly *her* fault Zara preferred her company to that of Deborah More, but it would make life harder for the girl, Emma acknowledged. For Zara's sake she must not encourage her. She could not turn her away from the door but must certainly be cool and matter-of-fact about their relationship.

The following evening, just as Emma was pre-

paring to go on duty at the hospital, there was a
sharp tap at her door. Making sure the chain was in
place, she opened it a crack, to see Dr Matthew's
burly figure outside. Hesitantly, she let him in, or at
least, she invited him in, but he came no farther
than the threshold.

His sleepy, blue-grey gaze swept dispassionately
over her. 'Going out, Mrs Nichols?'

She nodded. 'It does me good to get out of here.
The same four walls every evening begin to pall
after a while.'

'I've got the car outside. Mrs Parry can't do
evening surgery. Her daughter's ill and she's having
her grandchildren to stay.'

'Yes?' Emma was sorry about Mrs Parry's
daughter but couldn't see that it concerned her.
Then the penny dropped. She was wanted for
evening surgery!

'Oh, no! I can't, Doctor. I'm sorry,' she said
nervously.

'Sorry! What good is that? Ruth can't cope alone
and one of the receptionists has gone down with the
bug. You will have to divide your time between the
two jobs.'

'Two jobs?' she queried. 'How did you hear
about the other one? Oh, I see what you mean,' she
hurried on, but he moved nearer, menacingly so.

'What other one, Mrs Nichols? Are you telling
me you have an evening job as well?'

'Yes, I have,' she said defiantly. 'There's no law
against it, surely?'

'No,' he conceded, a muscle at the corner of his
jaw working angrily. 'But you were employed on

the understanding that you would be available to work evenings when required.'

'Only in exceptional circumstances,' she insisted.

'These *are* exceptional circumstances,' he put in, and Emma had to admit he was right.

She was needed in both places. They were short of staff at the hospital, too, but her first priority was to the health centre.

Sighing, she told him she would be along later. 'Later? Why not now? I can run you in.'

'You won't be able to bring me back,' she said calmly. 'You have visits after surgery.'

'You can come, too. Be a change from whatever you generally do in the evenings,' he said sharply. 'What is it, anyway? Barmaid? Bingo-caller? Topless waitress?' he suggested, and her face burned.

'I'm hardly the build for a topless waitress,' she pointed out. 'Or a barmaid, come to that.'

He eyed her speculatively. 'Perhaps not. A bit dowdy, too,' he added, and Emma's eyes blazed.

'You're a pig of the lowest order!' she snapped, but he chuckled.

'Shouldn't it be highest order?' he suggested facetiously, and Emma almost slammed the door in his face.

She couldn't stand the man! 'Why are you so hateful to me!' she cried, uncaring whether he replied or not. 'Is it fun to pick holes in me, criticise my every move, make spiteful remarks about my appearance? Does it make you feel good, Dr Matthew?' she almost screeched.

'Shh! Your neighbours will think I'm killing you,'

he said gently, smoothing a lock of golden hair out of her eyes—eyes that were bright with tears.

'Oh, Emma!' he almost choked out her name, then swiftly recovered himself. 'I'll wait in the car,' he went on brusquely, and hastened away.

Tears ran unchecked down her face as she quietly closed the door after him. Now she understood. She loved him! All the dislike, all the arguments, were as nothing compared with this!

She, Emma Nichols, grieving widow, loved one Dr Matthew Scofield, a widower with a teenage daughter. A widower with an intelligent and attractive fiancée. And her love was not returned even though, for a moment there, she'd thought he cared a little for her.

Probably he was tired and needed some tender loving care. That was all. She was almost certain he'd been about to sweep her into his arms. That choked-off way he spoke her name, the muscle working at the corner of his jaw, the expression in his eyes . . .

She sank on to the settee and covered her face with her hands. She was a fool to think it meant anything. But, yes, she did love him. There was no doubt of that.

As she raised her head, her gaze fell upon the old rocking-chair—Tony's rocking-chair, and guilt overwhelmed her. She loved Tony, so how could she love Matthew? There was no answer to that question, and she avoided looking at the chair while she gathered up her things, banging the door behind her.

She must telephone the hospital and explain her

absence. But explaining this strange, unrequited love was a different matter. It was something shoddy, to be put out of her mind completely.

As she settled herself next to Dr Matthew, and he impersonally fastened the seat-belt about her, she knew putting him out of her mind was not only difficult, it was impossible.

She would have to leave the health centre. Perhaps she could work full-time as an auxiliary until accepted for training.

'Mrs Drummond is first on my list after surgery,' Dr Matthew was saying, and Emma tried to concentrate as he discussed the patients he would be calling on that evening.

All the while her new knowledge weighed heavily upon her. I love Matthew, I love Matthew, the car-engine seemed to be saying as they drove along. She was glad to see the health centre entrance, glad to get out of the car, away from his disturbing presence.

Evening surgery was packed, as she'd expected, and by the time she'd shown in the last coughing, sneezing patient she didn't feel all that well herself! A doctors' receptionist was exposed to all kinds of bacteria and she supposed it was only a matter of time before she came down with something, particularly in her present weakened state. Her appetite was still negligible and she was overworking her slender body.

She was depressed, too, and slept badly despite her tiredness.

'We've only five visits,' Dr Matthew told her as he led the way to his car after surgery.

'Only five! It sounds enough,' she said lightly, pleased by the way he said 'we' rather than 'I'. It made her feel she was a partner in his healing, rather than a mere receptionist who could do no more than basic nursing or first aid.

'What's wrong with Mrs Drummond?' she asked as he set the car in motion. 'I saw her three or four days ago. We had tea together.'

'Her neighbour phoned. That odd old fellow who lives next door.'

Emma smiled, recalling the suspicious eyes and the wizened face only too well.

'He had some reason to knock on her door, apparently, and couldn't get a reply, so he called the health visitor. Mrs Smith went this afternoon and thinks the old girl ought to be in a home.'

'No!' Emma protested. 'She's a bit eccentric but she manages. And what about her cat?'

'That mangy ginger cat? I don't know. Perhaps you could look after it for a while?' he suggested.

The idea wasn't appealing, and she could hardly keep it cooped up in her room all day, but it might have to come to that.

They hammered on Mrs Drummond's door but to no avail. Then Matthew miraculously produced a key from his pocket and, to Emma's astonishment, unlocked the door.

'She gave the spare key to Mrs Smith. Reluctantly,' he explained as they entered the dingy room.

Because of the drawn curtains Emma could see nothing at first, then something furry brushed past her leg and she squealed. Out of the gloom Mrs

Drummond's voice came, demanding querulously to know who they were.

Emma hurried over to reassure her while Dr Matthew attempted to switch on the light.

'Bulb's gone,' Mrs Drummond croaked, clutching Emma's hand as a spasm of coughing overtook her.

Knowing how deaf she was, Emma pointed to the light socket which she could see now that she'd adjusted to the dimness. Understanding her, Mrs Drummond rummaged about in a large brown paper bag by the bed and produced a low-watt light bulb which the doctor inserted.

Adequate but poor light flooded the room and they saw that Mrs Drummond was muffled up in numerous shawls and rugs. The electric fire was on full and the room was stuffy. Emma was tempted to switch it off and open the sash window, but resisted the urge.

Dr Matthew, meanwhile, was busily taking Mrs Drummond's pulse and temperature. 'You don't seem too bad,' he said loudly, and the woman smiled, revealing a few yellowed teeth.

'Sorry I couldn't come before,' he went on. 'Had a busy day.'

She nodded vigorously. 'I've had a busy day, too. Been tidying my tins, Doctor.' She pointed to the tins of paint which had been neatly stacked along one side of the wall.

'Very nice,' he commented, then wrote out a prescription.

When Mrs Drummond saw it she shook her head. 'Got my own stuff. Swear by it, Doctor.' She indicated a small meat-safe in the corner and Emma hurried to open it.

Bottles of medicine were tidily arranged on the lower shelf, while the upper one held bottles of tablets and capsules.

Half-amused, half-horrified, Emma found the cough medicine and a bottle of expectorant and took them across to the doctor. Then, despite Mrs Drummond's protests, Emma obeyed Dr Matthew's instructions to gather up all the pills and potions.

'If they aren't too old and might be useful to her, leave them,' he ordered. 'Any antibiotics must be destroyed. You can be clearing things up here while I make my next couple of visits. I'll call back.'

He was gone before Emma could protest. He had certainly set her a difficult task. She didn't think it was her place to dispose of the patient's unwanted medicine but gathered together what was no longer of use. The chemist would get rid of them tomorrow.

Mrs Drummond was cross but resigned by now, and Emma smiled at her frequently, since conversation was so difficult.

The ginger cat returned before Dr Matthew, and a relieved Mrs Drummond held out her arms to it. The old lady seemed better now, and Emma mimed the act of cooking. She was boiling an egg when Matthew came to fetch her, and it was agreed she would settle Mrs Drummond for the night while he carried on with his rounds.

He hesitated before leaving. 'Are you sure you will be all right?'

He sounded concerned, and a faint pink flush tinged her cheeks. If only he was concerned because he cared about her, not just because he felt guilty at leaving her to do some unexpected voluntary work.

'I'll get a taxi when I've finished, Doctor,' she said crisply. 'There's bound to be a telephone somewhere.'

'No! It's not a very salubrious neighbourhood, even in broad daylight. Stay here till I get back,' he ordered.

Pleased because he cared for her well-being, Emma busied herself giving Mrs Drummond her supper, then tidied up quickly, not wanting to waste Matthew's time when he returned. When he did, he produced a couple of capsules and a vigilant Emma stood over Mrs Drummond to make sure she swallowed them.

When they left they took the prescription away with them, Emma having promised to drop the medication in the following day. Dr Matthew would make arrangements for the nurse to visit to see that the old lady was going on all right.

'She isn't too bad,' he commented as they headed away from the area. 'A bit chesty, but she'll do. I wouldn't dare broach the subject of a nursing home!' he chuckled, and Emma joined in.

She felt warm and cherished, sitting beside him, listening to him talk about his evening's visits. She was sorry when they reached her house, half hoping that he would take her home to King's House.

But that was a foolish dream. She had helped him and she supposed he was grateful. By tomorrow he would have forgotten all about it, be his usual aloof self.

But to Emma's surprise, his attitude towards her changed after that evening. He expressed the wish that she and Zara might resume their former friendship, and a delighted Emma found herself invited to visit Zara at home whenever she wished.

The first opportunity came the following week. Emma took her to an afternoon play given by a local theatre group in the newly-built library theatre. Afterwards, Zara insisted on taking Emma home to tea and they sat on the sunlit patio eating home-made scones and drinking tea.

Emma sighed contentedly. So much space, so much fresh air and sunlight. The weather had changed yet again. Although it could not be called hot it was certainly warm and Emma wore only a cardigan over her striped summer dress. She would be glad of her jacket later because the evenings rapidly turned chilly.

King's House boasted an enormous garden, much of it wild and overgrown, though Zara told Emma that her father had hired a man with a rotovator to break up the soil. Nothing much grew there save a mass of weeds, some of them rather pretty. Emma could not recall where she had heard the remark that a weed was merely a flower in the wrong place, but there was a lot of truth in it.

Suddenly Zara jumped up and rushed into the house, and a perplexed Emma was about to follow when the girl returned, arm in arm with her father. Acutely conscious that she was as dowdy as ever, Emma smiled briefly at the doctor, then resumed her seat and reached for her empty cup so as to have something to hold on to.

His sharp eyes didn't miss the self-conscious gesture, and a sad smile drifted across his face.

'Run along for a while, there's a pet,' he instructed his daughter. 'I want to speak to Mrs Nichols.'

Cold hands seemed to clutch at Emma's heart as the girl tripped away, singing to herself. What fault was being laid at her door this time? she wondered, her expressive blue eyes fixed on the man she loved.

CHAPTER EIGHT

HAVING got rid of his daughter, Dr Matthew seemed uncertain how to begin.

Emma, sitting with her arms folded, her ankles neatly crossed, wasn't disposed to help him. Whatever he wanted to say, it would not be to her advantage.

He cleared his throat and his long fingers eased the subdued blue necktie, and still Emma waited.

'Have you settled in all right?' His voice was strained and she looked up, her expression anxious.

'Yes, thank you, Doctor,' she said meekly. 'I enjoy working at the health centre.'

'And your other job? Is that going well?' he went on conversationally, settling himself opposite her in the wicker chair. Their feet accidentally touched and Dr Matthew shot up as though stung, and commenced pacing up and down the patio.

Startled, Emma said yes, her other job was going well. 'So well,' she added cautiously, 'that I might do it full-time. Leave the centre, I mean.'

She would have to, sooner or later. She couldn't stand being so near to the man she loved and seeing him fall more and more under the spell of the green-eyed Deborah.

'Leave!' he exploded, ceasing his restless pacing and coming to stand before her. His eyes were anguished, more grey than blue now.

'Well, yes. I always thought that one day I would return to nursing.'

'Nursing? Is that your other job?'

'Mm. I'm an evening auxiliary at the hospital. It's not really nursing,' she admitted, wondering why he should care either way.

'Nursing,' he repeated. 'I tried to imagine what you did in the evenings, but I never thought about nursing.'

'Was it your place to wonder, Doctor?' she asked, annoyed. 'I should have thought my private life was my own concern.'

'Yes, of course,' he murmured, still staring down at her, his expression strained. 'No! It's my concern as well!'

'Is it? Why?'

'Because . . . because I like to know what the staff do in their spare time,' he said awkwardly, and Emma's eyes glinted with anger.

'I might like to know what *you* do in your spare time but I wouldn't ask!' she retorted rashly, and a delighted smile lit the doctor's face.

'Do you want to know?' he asked softly, drawing her up to face him. Confused, Emma nodded, then tried to shake her head. What was she admitting to?

Before she could assure him that she wasn't the tiniest bit interested in his private life, her lips were claimed in a long, hungry kiss. All coherent thought left her for a few moments, those few precious moments before he cast her aside with a violence that shocked her.

'Oh, Emma!' he cried brokenly, reaching for her again but, panicking, she stood behind the wicker chair.

If he was angry at his own weakness, sorry he had kissed her, that was *his* problem. She would not be used, picked up and put down again as though she was a toy.

Before she could give him a piece of her mind, Zara came rushing out.

'Daddy, Daddy! There's a man at the door. There's been an accident! On the road!' She clutched at her father's sleeve and he hurried away.

It took a moment for Emma to compose herself, bring her mind back to the mundane present. Then she, too, rushed through the house and out the front door, her thoughts now on the accident.

There had been a three-car pile-up. They hadn't heard it because it was just on the bend and some way past Matthew's house. Luckily, a passer-by knew where he lived.

The police were there by the time Emma arrived, hobbling because she'd lost her sandal and trodden on some loose gravel.

'A police car was chasing one of the others,' Zara told her, eyes wide with excitement. 'I don't think anyone is dead.'

Emma hastened to help and was nearly at Dr Matthew's side when she was pushed rudely away, a voice she knew well saying, 'Let me through! I'm a doctor.'

Deborah More joined Matthew, and Emma hovered indecisively for a moment until she saw that she could still be of use. One of the victims was holding a hankie to her cut brow, and Emma went to tend to her.

It was only a superficial cut, as were most of the injuries, a miracle indeed, and swiftly it was all over.

The ambulance departed with the driver and front-seat passenger of one vehicle, and Emma saw Matthew take Deborah's arm as they left the scene, having done all they could. Even Zara had disappeared, and a forgotten Emma was left, watching Matthew and Deborah get into Deborah's car and drive away.

They could not see her, for there were a great many people still hovering about. Even so, Matthew might have remembered her, ought to have looked for her. He did not know she'd followed him, she realised, but surely he would expect her to try to help?

She retraced her steps until she found her other sandal, then noticed the blood on her dress, presumably from the lady with the lacerated brow.

Luckily she had thought to bring her shoulder-bag with her, for in addition to the small first aid kit, it also held her purse. She had enough money to get home.

Her car was at King's House but she did not feel up to facing Dr More just now. And she certainly did not feel disposed to see Dr Matthew.

Later that evening Dr Matthew hammered at her door. She edged it open, almost certain it was him. His angry, set face confronted her, and she reluctantly let him in.

'Where were you?' he demanded, catching hold of both her hands and holding them tightly.

Heart fluttering, Emma stammered out that she'd tried to help, then returned home.

'Why didn't you come back home with me?' he asked, belligerently, his grip tightening.

'Let go of me! You're hurting!' she squealed, but he took no notice.

'You went off with Dr More!' she snapped. 'I was left standing there like . . . like a lemon!'

'I can't see what lemons have to do with it,' he said testily. 'I didn't know you were there. Why on earth didn't you call after me? Am I such an arrogant boor that I would leave you in the road?' His tone was anguished, but Emma hardened her heart.

'You might if the fancy took you,' she charged, jealousy of Deborah More goading her. 'I'll pick up my car tomorrow if that's all right,' she added hastily, sensing the leashed anger in him. She could not afford to try his patience too far, he had a short fuse where she was concerned.

'Are you jealous of Deborah?' he asked, his voice deceptively soft, and Emma flushed. His remark was spot-on and she was a hopeless liar.

'No, of course not. What has she got that I want? That is the basis of jealousy, isn't it?'

'I suppose so,' he acknowledged. 'You aren't jealous of my friendship with her, then?'

Emma almost choked. He was too perceptive! Indignantly she denied it. 'I didn't return to the house with you because I thought myself surplus to requirements!' she added, wanting to hurt him as he had hurt her. 'Dr More doesn't like me, anyway.'

'Nonsense! You are a pig-headed little fool and I ought to put you over my knee and spank some sense into you!' he exploded, eyes a stormy grey.

They glared at each other and Emma wanted to cry. Why was it that whenever they set out to hold a conversation, they ended up yelling at each other like harridans?

She asked him that question, brokenly, but he shook his head.

'I don't know, Emma. It's strange, isn't it? We aren't meant to hold a conversation, perhaps. We could be engaged in quite a different activity.'

She opened her mouth in surprise, and saw his eyes fixed greedily upon her.

'No,' she whispered, the four walls of the room coming to meet her, closing in upon her just as Matthew was doing.

'Don't say no to me, Emma,' he whispered huskily, reaching out for her.

She met him half-way, pressing her body against his, wanting to be as near to his heart as possible. She knew it was simply desire on his part, that he did not love her. Yet he wanted her. That much was evident.

Desire might be enough. All the love was on her side but she wanted him, too. Desire overwhelmed her, an eagerness to be his completely, and she felt deliciously faint.

'Emma, Emma,' he said, over and over again. 'Emma, I need you.' Not love but need. Never mind, she wasn't greedy. She loved him, that was sufficient justification for giving her all.

His hands caressed her into a frenzy of desire, until she could hardly stand. 'Matthew, I lo . . .' she began, then hastily closed her mouth, only to have her lips forced apart by the pressure of his.

A lucky escape. She had so nearly told him she loved him. Then her mind emptied itself of all except her love and her need for this arrogant, masterful man.

He swept her into his arms and she made no protest when he put her gently down on the bed-settee. And then the rocking-chair came into view. Tony's rocking-chair! Guiltily, she flung Matthew away.

'Emma, what's wrong? Don't say no, please.' His deep voice was choked, and Emma's heart almost broke.

'I can't, Matthew. I can't. I'm sorry. It's the chair,' she half-sobbed.

He lifted incredulous eyes to hers. 'The rocking-chair?'

She nodded, holding her hands up to her flushed face. 'It's Tony's. *Was* Tony's. It's staring at me, making me feel guilty,' she whispered, doubting that a man would understand such a feeling.

Yet he seemed to, and rose heavily, his eyes still upon her flushed face. In them she saw desire—desire that she supposed was mirrored in her own.

'I feel guilty as well,' he admitted with a wry smile, and she knew what he meant.

Deborah More. He had no business making love to other women. It wasn't fair to the woman he really loved.

Absently he patted her shoulder, a fatherly gesture more than a lover-like one, then left quietly. There was a vacuum in the room, an emptiness. Just like the emptiness in Emma's heart.

Emma had a new patient to visit now, a Miss Amelia Butler. She was a short, very thin, rather wizened lady with an unfortunate, off-putting manner.

Her attitude towards Emma was haughty. She had held a position of responsibility during her working years until ill-health forced her into an early and bitterly resented retirement, and she took out her resentment on Emma.

She was one of Dr Partington's patients, and he had asked Dr Matthew if he would get Emma to visit, see what she could do for the woman. Miss Butler did not need a nurse to keep an eye on her, merely a regular visitor to see that she was coping.

During her visits Emma tried desperately hard to persuade her to join the local club for the elderly, but Miss Butler's pale eyes flashed indignantly. 'Join in with all those slovenly people!' she exclaimed. 'Some of them don't take a proper bath, I'll have you know.'

'Some of them can't manage to get *into* a bath,' Emma explained, trying to hold on to her temper. It wasn't easy for Miss Butler to accept help of any kind, even a voluntary visitor, and Emma knew that it would take only one unkind word from her and the proud old woman would order her out of the bungalow.

'*I* manage,' Miss Butler said proudly, getting up to show that the visit was over. She had arthritis and could barely hobble to the door to let Emma out.

Emma was surprised to be called in to see Dr Partington the next day and stunned at what he had to say.

She was being accused of stealing Miss Butler's purse! Shock went over her in waves as she stood in front of Dr Partington's desk.

'I didn't see a purse in the sitting-room, Doctor,' she assured him. 'Probably she put it somewhere for safety and forgot where she left it.'

'I've no doubt of that, my dear,' he hastened to assure her. 'But facts are facts. An accusation has been levelled against you and I have to act accordingly.'

Emma nodded, not really understanding. Then the blow fell.

'I'm afraid you will have to curtail your visits—just for the time being,' the old doctor said, shrewd grey eyes on Emma's unnaturally pale face.

Wearily she pushed back a lock of gold hair, her hand trembling. 'Then I am being presumed guilty,' she said shakily.

'No, no, my dear! Nothing of the sort!' he snorted. 'But you know how it is. We are all in a vulnerable position. Whatever a doctor or nurse does can be blown up out of all proportion. The slight misdemeanour, the merest suspicion,' he hurried on.

That much was true. She supposed it was fair. Once the old lady found her purse she could resume visiting, though she did not feel inclined to call upon Miss Amelia Butler again!

The woman appeared not to like her, and one accusation was enough. Let someone else visit in future.

Unfortunately the ban also applied to visiting Mrs Drummond, who looked forward eagerly to Emma's calls.

When she protested about that, Dr Partington reddened. 'I'm very sorry, Emma, but there it is.' He hesitated, then went on bluntly, 'If it was up to a certain member of staff, you would be asked to leave the health centre altogether.'

Emma could not believe her ears. Condemned without a trial, simply on the word of a forgetful old woman!

For a moment she couldn't find words, but one name leapt into her mind. Matthew! It must be he who wanted rid of her.

How could he? It would relieve him of their daily meetings, which he now found embarrassing. Since the day of the road accident, the evening he and Emma had so nearly made love, his manner had resumed its usual aloofness. He was never nasty or sharp with her, as in days gone by, but they were as distant as ever.

He never smiled at her now or asked her opinion about any of the old folk she visited, though she knew he still consulted her carefully-filed notes from time to time. This must be his way of disentangling himself, goaded no doubt by Deborah More.

Hurt beyond measure, Emma stumbled from the surgery. Head bent, she stood at the top of the short flight of stairs, wondering if she had the heart to go on. Would it not be better to resign now?

That would be an admission of guilt. To go whilst under a cloud of suspicion would be most unwise. Yet could she continue, knowing how keen Matthew and Deborah were to be rid of her? Might they not find other ways of easing her out of the job?

'Emma?' Matthew's voice sounded strangely hesitant.

He stood at the bottom of the stairs, and she glared down at him.

'Come to gloat, have you?' she snapped, as the tears started to fall.

She hurried down the stairs, trying to avoid his outstretched arms, but found herself imprisoned. His arms tightened about her and she laid her weary head upon his shoulder and wept.

'How could you?' she kept moaning. 'How could you do this to me?'

He was hateful, despicable! Savagely she pushed against his chest, and a bemused Matthew let her go.

She rushed past him to the privacy of the staff lavatory. There, at least, he could not follow.

It was half day at the surgery but Emma was, not surprisingly, behind with her work. After the trauma of the morning she could not get into her routine and she was wearily filing record cards in the reception area when Dr Matthew strode through the main doors later.

She barely glanced up. She knew it was him, for she'd seen his car draw up outside. Whatever he wanted, she wasn't interested.

'Are you nearly finished, Emma?' he asked

crisply, fingers drumming impatiently upon the counter.

She gave him a level look. 'No. I'm rather behind. Excuse me, I have a lot to do.'

'That can wait!' he snapped. 'You and I are going to call upon Miss Butler.'

'Why?' she cried. 'You have made up your mind I'm guilty! Am I supposed to go down on bended knee and beg the old witch's forgiveness?'

'Have I?' He sounded genuinely surprised, and uncertainty darkened her eyes.

'You told Dr Partington I should be dismissed!' she charged. 'Didn't you?' she went on, but wasn't surprised when he shook his head.

'Then it must have been Dr More,' she said slowly, all becoming clear to her.

'Does it matter now? No one believed you to be a thief. Miss Butler wants to apologise. Are you going to be so proud and stiff-necked you won't come to accept her apology?'

'No! Of course I'll come, willingly.' She felt overjoyed at the sudden reversal. Presumably the old lady had found the purse. When, on the way to Miss Butler's bungalow, she suggested this, he shook his head.

'Not so. I called on her after morning surgery and read her the riot act! She still hadn't found the purse. Had her door-key in it, too.'

'Then . . . then how does she know I didn't steal it? She might be apologising to a thief for all she knows!'

He chuckled. 'Let's say I used my powers of persuasion. I knew you wouldn't have taken it and although I didn't want to twist her arm, I managed to make her see that she could have lost it elsewhere. After the initial fuss I think she felt guilty.'

The heavy cloud that settled on Emma earlier, lifted. Dr Matthew had believed in her enough to assure Miss Butler that she wasn't a thief! He must care for her a little, surely? Even a little would be enough.

So long as he cared about her, she could stand the strain of his engagement and marriage to Deborah, although an official announcement seemed to be a long time coming.

Miss Butler greeted them cordially, though she refused to meet Emma's candid blue gaze. Obviously embarrassed, she offered them tea. But Matthew had visits to make before he could go home for his lunch, and they refused.

'Has your purse turned up yet?' Emma asked gently, hoping to help the proud old woman.

She nodded, and they let out a sigh of relief. She pointed to the sideboard and Emma saw a big black notecase lying on top.

'That's it. I tucked it under a cushion out of sight when you came to the door, Mrs Nichols,' Miss Butler admitted. 'I wish to apologise for my accusation.'

She coloured fiercely, and Emma longed to comfort her. But she knew it would be unwise, might appear patronising.

'I accept your apology,' she assured her. 'I'm glad the purse has turned up.'

'Your fiancé almost wiped the floor with me,' Miss Butler went on quietly, and Emma opened her mouth to protest, but the old lady went on. 'He told me that you were the girl he was going to marry, and he wouldn't marry a thief. "You ought to be ashamed of yourself, Amelia Butler," he said. And I am,' she admitted, getting up slowly, lines of pain etched into her face.

She patted Emma's hand awkwardly before letting them out, and a stunned Emma made arrangements to call there at the weekend. She didn't know quite what to say to Dr Matthew. Mere words were inadequate. He had lied to save her reputation. If ever Miss Butler found him out in that lie, she might make trouble, even though she had been in the wrong herself.

'Thought you might come to lunch.' Matthew himself broke the silence.

Emma was about to refuse, but his next words threw her. 'I meant it, you know. About marrying me. Will you?'

His eyes were on the road and Emma had no idea what emotion showed in them, if any.

Marriage! She was being asked to marry Dr Matthew Scofield! Mrs Matthew Scofield. She started to speak several times but couldn't get the words out.

'Lost your ability to speak, Emma?' He sounded amused, and Emma blushed.

Already he was poking fun at her. How gauche and unsophisticated she must appear after Deborah More.

'You have a fiancée!' she burst out. 'Dr More.'

'She is not and never has been my fiancée,' he said coldly. 'We're here,' he added, and stopped the car to unlatch the double gates of his house.

'Home,' he said, as he got back into the car and drove in, leaving the gates open.

Home. The word echoed in Emma's tired brain. King's House would be her home . . . But she couldn't marry Matthew! She couldn't.

She tried to tell him so but he wouldn't listen. 'Later, Emma. Jump out, there's a good girl. I have several visits before I can eat. Mrs Fillery will look after you.'

Emma found the housekeeper eyeing her quiz-zically as she stood watching Matthew's car disappear down the drive. She was to become Matthew's wife—Zara's stepmother.

Pulling herself together, a dazed and shaken Emma followed Mrs Fillery into the sitting-room and sank on to the velvet settee. Her legs were no longer capable of supporting her.

'Will you be wanting lunch now, Mrs Nichols? Or will you wait for the doctor?' Mrs Fillery asked in hushed tones.

Emma told her she would wait for Matthew and the tall, portly housekeeper withdrew, closing the door quietly behind her.

From her curious glances, Emma guessed that the woman knew. But she couldn't know about the engagement. Matthew had only just asked her! Yet Miss Butler knew, even before the intended bride.

Indignation overcame her and she jumped up, wishing she could find something on which to vent her anger. She was too angry even to feel the pangs of hunger, and wandered about the big room, touching a painting here, an ornament there.

All this would be hers if she accepted Matthew's proposal. She would become mistress of King's House.

She wasn't poor, in any case. She had what remained of the selling price of their old home. But this was luxury even compared with the house she and Tony had shared.

And that lovely, wild garden! That would become hers, as well.

Stop it, Emma! she told herself. You're becoming mercenary. You can't marry Matthew. He doesn't love you.

That was true, she reflected bitterly. Whatever his reason for marrying her, it wasn't love.

There was another thing. Barely eighteen months had passed since her husband's death. It would not be fair to his memory to remarry so soon, if at all.

For she had genuinely loved Tony. True, he was often selfish and very possessive, but she hadn't minded that much. Their marriage was strong and could withstand such vicissitudes.

Yet if truth be told, she was now enjoying the independence he had tried to take from her. Did she want to become another man's chattel? If that man was Matthew Scofield the answer must be yes!

Still she hesitated, mulling over the exact wording of her reply. She was so lost in thought that she didn't hear Matthew return. He was in the room before she knew it, and she eyed him warily, hoping he would not make any move towards her.

'Sorry I'm so late,' he apologised briefly. 'Will you marry me, Emma? Give Zara a mother's care and the security she has never known?'

His smile was winsome, his heavy-lidded eyes pleading with her. In a way she was relieved. Now she knew the reason for the proposal. It was because he thought she would make a better mother for his daughter than Dr Deborah More.

At least she could try. Zara would be the daughter for whom she had longed. That there would never be brothers and sisters for Zara, she accepted. She had no doubt that Matthew would continue his love-affair with Deborah More.

That hurt, but perhaps some day he would turn to her for comfort, realise that there was enough love in his own home without seeking it elsewhere. One day he might even come to love her. She could only hope and pray.

'Yes, I'll marry you,' she said, her throat dry.

CHAPTER NINE

ZARA WAS thrilled, both by the engagement and by the gift of the rocking-chair.

The engagement she accepted without question, insisting that she would now call Emma 'Mother'.

About the rocking-chair she wasn't so sure. 'Do you really want me to have it?' she asked later that day.

Matthew had left them alone once Zara returned from school, merely telling his daughter that he and Mrs Nichols were to be married, if that was all right with her. Her delighted smile left the couple in no doubt of her thoughts on the matter, and Emma hugged her, almost choking with emotion.

She was to be part of a family. Perhaps not a real family, but the best she could hope for in the circumstances.

'Yes, I want you to take the rocker. If your father is agreeable,' Emma added, not sure he would approve. She must not usurp his parental rights. She was only to be a stepmother and he might be angered by the gift.

Perhaps, too, it was unwise. Far better to sell it; yet she'd tried to in the past and failed.

He might not be keen on the previous husband's possessions being brought into his home. But as he did not love her there was no real basis for his objection. He could hardly be said to be jealous.

And as it turned out, he accepted the gift without demur, which pleased Zara at least.

The wedding was to take place at the end of August and when Matthew suggested they honeymoon in the Channel Islands, Emma was delighted. Together they chose Guernsey, since it would be quiet and restful. Emma hesitantly suggested they might take Zara, since it would be the school summer holidays, but Matthew put his foot down.

'There will be plenty of family holidays for us later,' he decreed. 'Zara will spend a few days with my father.'

Since it was for Zara's sake the marriage was taking place at all, Emma felt bound to protest. When she pointed that out to him, he looked uncomfortable.

Still he refused to change his mind, and luckily Zara did not expect to go with them. After she'd dwelt on the matter a while, Emma realised Matthew needed a break from the girl. He was a hard-working GP who needed to relax completely on holiday. He could hardly do so if he was constantly worrying about Zara, wondering if she was bored. Wondering, too, whether she might get in with some undesirables.

With his father she would be safe. Old Dr Scofield had a daughter, Jessica, who had a young family, and Zara might be happier with her cousins.

It was only for a fortnight, anyway. Two weeks. A two-week honeymoon without a wedding-night, Emma mused sadly, then quickly shut out the thought. She must not be greedy. She was to receive Matthew's name, his protection. That must be sufficient.

Of course, Matthew had to be introduced to her parents. They knew about the engagement and were pleased for their daughter, and most anxious to meet Matthew.

And he soon charmed them. After a few moments awkwardness they were soon completely at their ease with their new son-in-law and granddaughter. Zara was delighted to have two new grandparents, and hung on their every word.

Emma, watching discreetly, was relieved. It had to be said that her parents got on better with Matthew than she herself did. Zara was a pet so far, but was wilful and headstrong and Emma didn't doubt that there would be problems with her over the next year or two. It was a relief to know that her parents would provide support if necessary.

Neither of them had ever really liked Tony, she reflected later as Matthew drove them back home. Indeed, in a snatched moment of privacy that day, her mother had made sure Emma was aware of their feelings about Tony. He had been weak and selfish and far too possessive, she had said firmly.

When Emma, shocked, had protested, her mother relented a little and said it wasn't fair to speak ill of the dead and that probably Tony's upbringing had something to do with his selfishness.

Emma sat in the back of the car with Zara and stared at Matthew's head as he drove them home. His hair was rather long at the back, yet it suited him. It was crinkly to the touch, she knew, though they hadn't been near each other since the engagement.

That was nearly three weeks ago. Three weeks and he hadn't as much as kissed her brow! Whatever desire he had once felt for her had ebbed. Perhaps he was content with Deborah now.

She, of course, had taken the engagement badly. She'd made the remark, in Matthew's hearing, that as Emma was so domesticated she supposed it was natural he should want her as a stepmother for Zara.

Matthew hadn't commented in Emma's presence, and the remark stung for some time. More so because he hadn't leapt to her rescue.

She shrugged inwardly. Hadn't she always fought her own battles? Being married to a busy doctor meant she must continue to do so, and she'd probably have Zara's battles as well.

Emma continued to work, mornings only, at the health centre. She had fallen in with Matthew's wishes that she should not be a working wife, that Zara needed a mother, someone who wasn't too busy at the end of the day to listen to the girl's problems.

That meant not only giving up her auxiliary nursing at the hospital but also shelving the resumption of her training, for the time being. Matthew had understood how keen she was to finish her training. He was also of the mind that no prospective nurse should be dissuaded from a career in nursing.

For the time being, though, he insisted Zara must come first. It was settled, however, that once she was a little older Emma might be able to take up some sort of training, perhaps the part-time training for State Enrolment.

And Emma wouldn't have much time for visiting her old ladies, either. It was a pity Mrs Drummond couldn't come to the small, quiet reception, but perhaps it was as well. Emma was determined that Mrs Drummond and all Matthew's patients should have a piece of wedding cake. Zara was making the cake with the enthusiastic help of her cookery teacher.

Matthew was organising the reception and the wedding itself, leaving Emma with only her wedding outfit to buy. As a widow she found it difficult to know what to wear. She finally settled on a sapphire blue suit, the material soft and filmy and patterned with tiny blue and white flowers.

Her ring, too, was blue. 'A sapphire to match your eyes,' was how Matthew put it, and she was surprised that he'd even noticed the colour of her eyes. It was small, neat and unobtrusive, but Emma thought it the most beautiful ring in the world.

She caught herself gazing at it often and was doing so just a few days before the wedding, as she sat in the waiting-room. Surgery was almost over. Then Matthew, as he sometimes did, would join her in the tea-room and snatch a few minutes conversation before going out on his rounds.

The ring flashed as she twirled it, a soft smile lighting her face. She was a fool to love a man who cared so little . . .

'I'd like to see Dr Matthew Scofield,' a young voice said breathlessly, and Emma glanced up, a self-conscious smile on her face.

The patient appeared no more than sixteen or so but was heavily pregnant. It was really too late to take any more patients but Emma didn't like to turn her away.

'You are a bit late. Dr Matthew doesn't usually accept patients who come in after ten . . .' Emma began, but the girl wasn't listening.

With a soft moan she collapsed in a heap at Emma's feet. Eyes wide with shock, Emma stood transfixed for a moment, then hurriedly rang through to Matthew.

Get a doctor first, she reasoned, then see what first aid you can offer. She might well be going into labour.

By the time she put the receiver down, Stephen Dutton was by the girl's side and Emma let out a sigh of relief.

'How is she?' she whispered, but he shook his head warningly as the girl's lashes fluttered open.

'Hello, Joyce,' he said uncomfortably, trying to keep his distance.

'Oh hello, Dr Dutton.' To Emma's shocked amazement, the girl sat up and clasped her arms about Dr Dutton's neck. Then Matthew appeared, bristling with anger at being disturbed when he saw that he wasn't needed.

'Hello, Joyce,' he said shortly as a white-faced Stephen Dutton disentangled himself. 'About due, is it?'

Joyce nodded. 'I'm getting pains and I knew you would help me.' Emma had sensed now that Joyce was one of the centre's 'problem patients', and her realisation was confirmed when she turned to Emma with an ingenuous smile. 'He offered to help me get rid of it but it seemed a shame.'

'Yes, of course,' Emma murmured, feeling that she'd come in half-way through a nightmare. Anyway, with two doctors around she would not be called upon to act as emergency midwife, thank goodness!

She remembered vaguely what one had to do. With a first baby there was adequate time but subsequent babies sometimes hurried into the world. Joyce didn't seem old enough to have other children, which was a relief.

Matthew was on the telephone now, while Stephen Dutton held tightly onto Joyce's hand trying to keep away from her embrace.

Emma, thankfully, got on with tidying her desk and knew she might have time to get a few letters typed while Matthew was busy. Then Dr Partington rang for her to take some dictation, and an irate Dr Bhunjun called to ask where his next patient was. He'd been waiting several minutes and no one had come in.

His annoyance vanished when he was told of the emergency, but Emma had to keep Dr Partington waiting, not wanting to leave until the midwife arrived from the annexe. Presumably Joyce would be transferred to hospital now.

Dr Partington almost snapped at Emma when at last she did get up to his office and she almost burst into tears. It was all too much. She wasn't a wailing type of woman but she couldn't take any more. The forthcoming marriage and the honeymoon, particularly the honeymoon, weighed heavily on her mind. That, together with all the extra work she'd undertaken and Joyce collapsing on her, was too much.

She wasn't aware of Matthew entering the old doctor's surgery. But she was aware of his words. They drenched her like a dip in the Arctic Ocean.

'For God's sake pull yourself together!' he snapped. 'You ought to be seeing to the patients, not having an attack of the vapours up here!'

'Oh!' She balled her fists, wishing he wasn't so big. If he'd been a smaller man she could have hit him!

'That's better,' he approved. 'Show them what you're made of, Emma.' He patted her shoulder in an avuncular fashion, then strode out, leaving a shaken and angry Emma to wipe her eyes and generally tidy up.

Pull yourself together, indeed! How much did he expect from her? She wasn't a mindless machine that would keep on running. She was flesh and blood, and she'd had enough. Dr Partington agreed with her and told her she ought to go home. She was in no fit state to work.

That was true enough. Her mind was so tired it wasn't functioning properly, but one fact did register. If she went home now, leaving all that work, Matthew would never forgive her. Quitting again, his expression would say, even if he never actually said so.

No! She would not quit. She could at least type Dr Partington's letters. Then there were the appointments to send out for the chiropody clinic.

If Matthew wanted her to pull herself together, then she would. She would never forget his words, never forgive his lack of understanding. And she was going to marry this unfeeling monster!

All her doubts and fears came creeping back. She had her independence, why should she exchange it for instant parenthood? If she did not marry Matthew she could think seriously about resuming her training. She could still be a friend and confidante to Zara. It wasn't as if she was abandoning the girl.

For a few minutes Emma seriously considered breaking off the engagement. She would be free, free! Marriage to Tony had been a burden, even though she loved him. Now she was about to exchange one form of imprisonment for another.

Having glimpsed freedom why was she so keen on shutting herself away again? Let Deborah More marry Dr Matthew. She would be far more suitable. Zara would suffer but she was young and resilient and would soon accept the inevitable. It wasn't as if Matthew loved her, either. If he did . . .

She closed her eyes wearily and gathered up her notes. There was work to be done and she'd wasted enough time.

As she worked she found herself thinking about Joyce. It was a change from dwelling upon her own unhappiness. She doubted if the girl was married, and perhaps she had no one to whom she could turn.

Hesitantly she asked Matthew about her that evening. They were to dine with some old friends of his, the Sheridans, and he picked her up nearly twenty minutes late without explanation.

His manner was cordial but no more than that. Certainly he appeared to have forgotten his unkind words of that morning, though Emma hadn't.

'Joyce? She's a problem child. Or was. She'll soon have a problem child of her own,' he said shortly, obviously not keen on discussing a patient when he was off duty.

Emma would not be denied. After all, Joyce had collapsed in front of her and she felt for the girl, lonely and seemingly abandoned by the father.

'Will the father marry her?' she persisted, and Matthew frowned, all his attention on the road.

'She *is* married. She fancied herself in love with Steve Dutton at one time, that's why she was transferred to my list. Since she's so unbalanced an abortion was suggested, but the advice fell on deaf ears, as you've seen. Stop prying into what doesn't concern you!'

Rebuffed, Emma sat back, pale and shaken. No, she definitely wasn't going to marry this man!

She wouldn't upset him by telling him so there and then. Later, after dinner, would be better.

The dinner-party went off well and Emma found Matthew's friends cordial enough. They seemed pleased that he was to remarry but she wondered if either of the women present had been friends of Celia's rather than his. It was better not to know.

At least she'd felt at home, she reflected, as they drove slowly back in the moonlight. And although she was no glamour-girl she didn't think her appearance had disgraced him. She wore a softly pleated dress in French navy and elegant high-heeled sandals she'd bought only the previous week. Her only jewellery was a slim gold watch and her engagement ring, but she'd taken the trouble to wear a little make-up, even though she still smarted from Matthew's unkind words of that morning.

Let him see she wasn't always dowdy, a drab little thing, she'd decided, some of her old spirit returning.

It was as the car drew up in front of her bed-sitter that she dropped her bombshell.

Nervously twisting the sapphire ring round and round, she said quietly, 'I can't marry you, Matthew. I'm sorry.'

There was a stunned silence, then Matthew laughed harshly. 'Is this a sudden decision? Did one of my friends upset you?'

She hastened to reassure him. 'No, it was nothing like that. They were all very charming—even though they must have been perplexed.'

'Perplexed?' He undid his seat-belt and eased himself around to face her. 'Why should they be perplexed, Emma?' He sounded weary and Emma hated herself for spoiling his evening. The poor man was tired. She was a bitch, deliberately stirring up trouble just to spite him.

She wanted to let the matter drop, not liking to feel she was being difficult, but he insisted on knowing.

'Well—they must wonder why you are marrying me. Celia was bright and . . . and sophisticated. Zara told me her mother was usually the centre of attention at parties.'

'When she'd had a drop too much to drink,' Matthew commented dryly.

'I can't marry you—I can't!' she rushed on.

'Nonsense. It's nerves. All brides are nervous.'

His tone sounded patronising and just then Emma could not see the injustice she was doing him. All she could hear was Matthew telling her to pull herself together, be a good girl, get on with the wedding . . . She exploded.

'I'm sick of you, Matt Scofield!' she screamed, raising her hand to strike him.

He did not try to parry the blow, and the resounding slap she gave him sounded unnaturally loud in her ears.

'Oh, Matthew!' she moaned softly, bitterly ashamed of her childish outburst. 'Matthew, I'm sorry.'

'As long as *you* feel better,' he said mildly.

Of course she didn't feel better, she felt much, much worse. Rather like a child who had smacked her mother in a babyish tantrum, then had mother kiss her better.

Tears ran down her thin cheeks, and Matthew laughed softly. 'Don't cry, little one. Here.' He produced a hankie and Emma wiped her eyes, too ashamed even to say thank you. How could she behave in that way? It was alien to her nature and she hoped Matthew wouldn't think he was marrying a shrew.

But he wasn't marrying her. Or, rather, she wasn't marrying him. Hadn't she just broken off the engagement?

Sorrowfully, she tugged at the sapphire ring, but

it was a tight fit and wouldn't come off. More tears flowed as she struggled with it, then Matthew's big strong hands closed over hers and his warmth permeated her chilled body and heart. When he gathered her into his arms she went willingly, raising her damp face for his kiss.

He murmured her name over and over again and Emma snuggled closer, wanting to be part of him, longing to be his completely. His kisses became more demanding, his mouth all-pervading and Emma moaned. 'Love me, please, Matthew,' she murmured, and then wished she hadn't. Mentioning love was foolish of her, even though she'd meant physical lovemaking and not necessarily the spiritual kind for which her poor heart clamoured, too.

With a groan he pushed her away, but gently, and she did not feel rebuffed. She still had stars in her eyes and knew if she could persuade him to spend the night with her she could make him love her in all senses of the word.

But he didn't need her and certainly did not love her, or else he would have succumbed to his natural instincts. It couldn't be that he was reluctant to anticipate their marriage. She was hardly a blushing, inexperienced young girl.

No, her chance had gone. Now he was his normal, slightly aloof self. A stranger, almost.

'Matthew—about the wedding,' she began, aware that they hadn't settled the matter.

'It will take place as arranged,' he said gently. 'You're tired, Emma. Everything will be all right.'

He still held her cold hands and his fingers tightened on hers for a second or two. 'Goodnight, sweet Emma. Dream of me.'

Once he had seen her safely indoors he left, and an emotionally drained Emma went to her lonely bed. Dream of me, he said. He couldn't know that she always did.

The week before the wedding passed in a whirl of activity. Each night a weary Emma went early to bed in search of the sleep she needed so badly. Yet each night she lay wakeful, falling asleep in fits and starts after hours of lying staring at the ceiling. Her dreams were vivid, most of them featuring Matthew. He was usually in a warlike mood and chased her along echoing corridors but he never actually caught her.

When the day of the wedding dawned she felt— and looked—anything but a radiant bride. Yet somehow she got through the day, making the correct responses during the quiet, civil ceremony.

Only her parents were there from her side. Zara and Matthew's father and sister, with her children, all came. Dr Partington was there but the other doctors were on duty. Deborah More was on leave, thank goodness.

Matthew's best man was his brother-in-law. Ruth Evans had been invited but was on holiday in Wales, which was a great pity. Emma was fond of the garrulous Ruth and would have been glad of her support on this special occasion .

The day passed. First the wedding, then the reception. After that, Emma still in her pretty blue suit, came the drive to Eastleigh Airport.

Matthew's father, a tall, grey-haired man full of old-world courtesy, drove them to the airport.

Matthew took after his father, though was bigger-built. In old Dr Scofield Emma could see Matthew in his sixties. Tall, slightly stooped, his thick glossy hair touched with grey yet still abundant, like his father's.

Oh Matthew, I love you so much, she said silently as the small plane took off for Guernsey that afternoon. You will never know just how much I love you. Would they, she wondered, still be together when Matthew retired from medicine? But, no. Zara would have long ceased to need a mother. Would probably be a mother herself, or even a grandmother by then.

A grandmother! She herself would be a sort of grandmother to Zara's children, and with that she must be content. If the boys had long-lashed, blue-grey eyes and black curly hair, she certainly would be content!

Guernsey was beautiful. A gem nestling in the blue, blue sea. The warmth hit Emma as they left the aircraft.

Their hotel was some distance from St Peter Port, the capital of Guernsey, and the taxi took them from the immaculate, modern airport through what seemed miles of countryside, with everywhere the ubiquitous greenhouses. The recession had hit the island badly, the taxi-driver told Matthew, and many of the greenhouses were empty, a sad waste.

Here and there Emma caught a glimpse of the tranquil sea and wished they were to stay nearer the coast, though nowhere in Guernsey was far from the sea. There were flowers everywhere and muted birdsong as they arrived at the intimate country hotel Matthew had chosen.

'This used to be a farmhouse,' he commented, taking her arm as they strolled up to the old house. 'Set in its own grounds.' He waved an arm expansively, but by now Emma was too overwrought to bother about the scenery.

When she was introduced as 'Mrs Scofield' Emma nearly panicked. Matthew's hand tightened imperceptibly on hers as they followed the receptionist to their room. The dye was cast. She was the second Mrs Matthew Scofield—for better or for worse.

CHAPTER TEN

THEIR ROOM was spacious and well furnished, with ample room for hanging clothes, far more than Emma needed. She believed in travelling light and a medium-sized suitcase held all her belongings for the two weeks.

Now, as she glanced at her clothes on their hangers, she wondered if she had misjudged her needs. The hotel wasn't large or pretentious and she assumed there would be no need to dress for dinner. Even so, she would naturally wish to change into something a little better for the evenings.

As Matthew's wife he might expect her to wear a different dress each day. The drab Mrs Nichols had let him down again, she mused miserably, as he disappeared in the direction of the connecting bathroom.

There were twin beds and they dominated the room. She judged them to be rather more than single bed size. Room enough for two? she wondered bleakly, but it was absurd. Matthew had no interest in his new wife. Now that he'd found a substitute mother for Zara he was content.

Dinner was excellent, a feast fit for any gourmet. The dining-room was small and cosy, the shape of the room lending the tables an intimacy, a privacy usually lacking in hotels.

Emma felt more comfortable now. Matthew was pleasant and chatty, having shed his usual aloofness the moment they reached the island. Here he was just a plain, ordinary tourist and he seemed to revel in his new role.

To Emma, he was attentive but not overwhelmingly so, and she relaxed. At least they could be friends. The honeymoon might be enjoyable, after all.

After the delicious meal of smoked salmon followed by a huge steak sautéd in red wine, Emma had no room for a pudding. They took their coffee out on to the terrace, the scent from some unseen night flower drifting back to them as they sat in a companionable silence.

Emma wore the navy pleated dress Matthew had seen once before when they dined with his friends, the Sheridans. Thoughtfully, she stirred her coffee, wondering whether he liked navy blue. She knew so little about his likes and dislikes, that was the trouble. If only she knew him better . . .

'What would you like to do tomorrow?' he asked, his tone friendly.

She smiled. She had no idea what kind of things he did on holiday. 'Have you made any plans?'

'None at all. I thought we would take each day as it came. See what takes our fancy.' He moved his chair nearer and Emma tensed.

'Do you like navy blue?' Even to her ears her voice sounded strained.

'Navy blue what?' He stared at her and Emma felt hot colour suffuse her cheeks.

'Colours. I just wondered what your favourite

colour was. I know so little about you!' she burst out, staring straight ahead.

He laughed softly. To Emma his laughter sounded mocking.

'Does it matter? We have plenty of time to get acquainted,' he put in mildly.

'Yes, that's true,' she murmured, wishing she was back in Penlow. Wishing she was still Mrs Emma Nichols, widow. He couldn't care less! He didn't think it important that they knew so little about each other. Does it matter? he'd said. To Matthew evidently it did not.

Bedtime came around much too soon for Emma. When Matthew suggested a drink at the bar before they turned in she responded eagerly and made her brandy last as long as possible.

By the time they went upstairs to their room, Emma was feeling quite light-headed, and the climb was an effort. Matthew gave her a searching glance as she stood in the doorway of their bedroom, smiling softly to herself. Then he swept her up in his arms and carried her over the threshold.

'Welcome, Mrs Scofield!' he said lightly, depositing her on the bed nearest the door. He sank down onto the other bed and removed his shoes, watched with a kind of detached interest by Emma.

Her head was spinning. She wasn't drunk by any means, but she certainly didn't feel right. She saw him pick up his quilted dressing-gown and head for the bathroom. A dark blue dressing-gown, she noted. He *did* like blue, then.

Pleased at this small discovery about her new husband, she sat up and swung her legs over the side of the bed. Dizziness forced her to abandon the attempt to get up, but she could at least undress.

All she remembered taking off was her dress, shoes and tights, then sleep claimed her. Bright morning sunlight wakened her and she lay there for a few seconds, trying to get her bearings.

She glanced up at the freshly emulsioned ceiling. It wasn't the one in her bed-sitter, that was for sure.

Then memory flooded back and she risked a shy glance at the other bed. It was empty.

Worried now, she sat up and rubbed her eyes. Matthew! Her wedding-night . . .

No, it wasn't a wedding-night. It was a farce. The whole marriage was a farce from start to finish. She began to cry, harsh sobs shaking her slender body.

Then Matthew was beside her, arms about her, comforting, protecting, soothing.

'Oh, Matthew!' she sobbed, resting her head against his broad shoulder. 'I'm so s—sorry.'

He didn't speak, merely drew her closer, and she closed her tired eyes, wishing it was for real, wishing he loved or desired her. He was merely being a good family doctor. Tender loving care, that was all it was. And she sobbed harder at the thought.

'Emma!' He shook her gently, then his hands slid down from her shoulders to her upper arms. Then they were about her waist, his fingers caressing, tantalising her body which was clad only in a short cotton nightie tied with a bow at the neck.

Her mind could not absorb this new information. She was sure she hadn't fully undressed before falling asleep last night. She recalled taking off her tights and dress, but . . .

'Matthew, no,' she whispered, still trying desperately to remember about last night. It seemed important.

Then the silk ribbon at her neck was being untied and she was pushed gently back against the pillow. Matthew was beside her, she found to her great surprise, and with infinite tenderness he eased the nightdress off her shoulders.

'Say yes, Emma,' he whispered seductively.

But she did not, could not speak, she was so choked with emotion. Instead, she opened her arms in welcome and with a cry Matthew came to her.

In their lovemaking Emma found the fulfilment that had always been denied her, for Matthew was not merely concerned with taking his own pleasure. He was a tender, considerate lover and she rose to heights of ecstasy greater than anything she had experienced before.

At last they slept as the morning sun rose higher, a blissfully happy Emma deciding that this was love, this was really love, before sleep overcame her and she snuggled closer to the man beside her.

It was nearly lunch-time when a drowsy Emma dragged herself to the bathroom, a smile still on her face. Of Matthew there was no sign, not even on the balcony which ran the whole length of their window.

She smiled even more as she recalled their morning's lovemaking. She ached deliciously and felt younger and more vital than she had ever done before. It seemed dreadfully decadent to spend a morning in bed, and it was a rare luxury for Emma.

She was busily making the bed, forgetting for a moment that it was an hotel and this would be attended to for them, when Matthew returned.

'I've arranged to lunch out,' Matthew's brisk, matter-of-fact voice startled her, and she turned to him with a shy smile.

His answering smile was formal, his eyes hooded, hiding his feelings, and she felt let down, chilled. He might have been a stranger standing there in the doorway, muscular arms folded. He was casually dressed in pale blue shirt and cords, and Emma felt overdressed in her cotton suit and court shoes.

'Where are we lunching?' She strove to keep her voice normal, calm, but it was an effort.

'I don't know yet. Thought we might stroll around, see what takes our fancy. There's a good bus service, if you'd rather?' he suggested, but Emma agreed that a walk would be more interesting.

'I'll change, though. I didn't know . . .' she faltered.

'Emma?' There was a question in his voice and she glanced up, wondering fearfully what was coming. 'About last night—this morning, rather.'

'Yes?' She forced coolness into her voice, trying to hide the hurt he had inflicted.

'I'm sorry. About taking advantage of you, I mean,' he hurried on, his tone defensive, and she gave what she hoped was a nonchalant laugh.

'It was nothing,' she assured him, and he flushed. 'I mean it was . . . there was no need to apologise. It was perfectly natural in the circumstances,' she hastened to assure him. 'Being our wedding-night.' Her voice broke on a sob, but she continued, not wanting him to offer false comfort, 'I understand, Matthew. Really. That you . . . you needed some-one.'

'A woman, do you mean?' His voice was danger-ously soft and she faltered before the glint in his eyes.

She nodded. 'Yes. It's perfectly all right. I . . . I didn't object.'

'Oh, good,' he said sardonically. 'I'm glad it wasn't too much of an ordeal for you. I'll wait in the lounge.'

Swiftly he was gone, and Emma stared at the empty doorway. I'm glad it wasn't too much of an ordeal, he'd said.

Oh, Matthew! her heart cried. If only you knew!

They took the bus after all, and lunched in St Peter Port. Matthew chose an unpretentious little restaurant where they ate seafood omelette with a huge salad.

Emma was too distressed to eat much and managed only half the omelette, pushing the rest of it away regretfully. What she'd eaten was delicious, and the salad was crisp and appetising. It wasn't a case of limp lettuce leaves and half a tomato. There were prawns, ham, peppers, tomatoes, olives, orange segments, potato and really crisp lettuce. In fact the salad alone would have made a meal and she was enthusiastic in her praise as they left.

They wandered around the shops for a short while but it was hot and crowded, and they soon found themselves at the harbour. A beautifully clean harbour, Emma noted. She stood still, breathing in the fresh sea air. This was paradise—or would be if only Matthew loved her.

'We might take the boat to Sark or Herm one day,' he suggested, and she turned to him, her face eager.

'That would be lovely, Matthew! I love the sea. Particularly when the sun glints on it.'

It was a perfect day with only the slightest of breezes, just enough to take the edge off the heat, and the sea was like a sheet of glass. She was glad now that she'd changed. The suit would have been unbearably hot.

'Shall we take a bus ride somewhere? Would you like that, Emma?' He was only inches from her, though he didn't touch her.

With a sad smile she said that whatever he wanted would be just fine with her.

Shrugging, he walked on, and Emma had to hurry to catch up. In the wrong again, she reflected bitterly, as she followed him from bus-stop to bus-stop while he decided where they should go.

They ended up near a small bay to the south of the island. The bus set them down at the top of a steep hill but Matthew discovered a footpath running parallel to the busy road, so he and Emma made their leisurely way down to the bay undeterred by the traffic.

Up above the road they could hear the cars passing as if from a great distance and when there wasn't any traffic the silence was almost tangible.

Emma stopped. 'Listen, Matthew,' she said shyly. 'You can hear the silence!' He wandered back, treating her to an enigmatic smile. He, too, listened. All about them there was this wonderful silence broken only by a bird chirping.

'It's an enchanted land, Emma. They set it up especially for us,' he joked.

She couldn't afterwards recall who made the first move, but in a moment they were in each other's arms. It seemed the most natural thing in the world for them to kiss in that enchanted place, free from prying eyes, away from all their worries and cares.

Natural, too, for them to stroll hand-in-hand the rest of the way down. Emma's face was alight with love and happiness.

She knew it was false hope that sustained her. Knew he could not possibly love her, but it didn't seem to matter at that moment. They were in paradise and nothing could spoil that.

They found themselves at the end of the cliff path overlooking the bay. By now it was high tide and only a few rocks were uncovered. To gain access to the beach they would have to use the steps cut into the cliff but decided against it. They could always return another day at low tide.

Emma gazed down at the swirling waters below. A stiff breeze sprang up and she was glad of the warmth of Matthew's protecting arm. She snuggled closer, half-afraid he might pull away, but he did not.

He chuckled and squeezed her gently. 'Come on, sleepyhead. Let's find a seat.'

Seats were plentiful and Emma sat down in some relief, easing the sandals off and wriggling her bare toes.

To her chagrin Matthew didn't sit beside her. Instead he settled himself on the grass and stretched out, closing his eyes.

They were sheltered from the wind by an outcrop of rock and Emma longed to throw herself on the grass beside her new husband, but didn't dare for fear of rejection.

Without warning, he caught hold of her feet and began to caress them, and she squealed.

'Matthew! Stop it! It tickles.' She cast a glance over her shoulder, embarrassed in case anyone should see them behaving like teenagers.

'Sorry,' he drawled, sounding anything but. Then he cradled one foot in his hands, his touch burning her.

He sat up and opened his mouth to speak, then closed his lips firmly, a rueful expression crossing his handsome face.

'Were you going to say something?' she enquired hopefully, but he shook his dark head.

'It wasn't anything of importance.' Then he glanced at his watch and got to his feet, looming over her.

'Time we were getting back. We don't want to miss another gourmet meal, do we?'

Reluctantly Emma rose. A small sigh escaped her as they retraced their steps. She would so have liked to spend the evening by the little bay.

Dinner was worth returning for, and the sea air and exercise gave Emma an appetite she didn't know she possessed. They started with melon, which slipped down easily enough, then Emma had a dish of scampi in an exotic sauce, plus salad.

Matthew settled for chicken cooked in wine with bacon, mushrooms and cream, a dish Emma decided she would have another evening. And they both finished with a sorbet followed by coffee topped with delicious Guernsey cream.

'A perfect end to a perfect day,' Matthew observed as they made their way upstairs much later, after a long walk around part of the hotel's extensive grounds.

Briefly, Emma wondered whether he was missing Deborah, though he gave no sign that he was brooding. Good food, fresh air and exercise seemed to fulfil him and if she didn't know better she would have assumed he actually enjoyed being with her. A substitute was better than no wife at all, she mused bleakly as Matthew again took his night-wear to the bathroom.

She undressed as quickly as she could, then wrapped her pink silk robe securely about her and waited till the bathroom was free. When he returned, humming a little tune, she hurried past, catching a whiff of his after-shave.

He was so masculine. All man, she thought wistfully, in his blue robe, its shortness displaying his long, muscular legs covered with fine dark hairs.

Longing overcame her and her heart started thudding in anticipation. In an effort to cool herself she splashed cold water vigorously over her body, then made liberal use of cologne.

Calm and in full control of her wayward feelings, she walked very slowly back into the bedroom. He would not want her in his arms tonight. Of that she felt sure, and she would not embarrass him by letting him see how much she cared. She had her pride. She tilted her chin a little higher, an unconscious gesture.

Matthew was in his own bed, his pyjama-clad arms clasped behind his head as he lay, seemingly lost in thought. His pyjamas were blue, too, she noticed as she moved gingerly towards the other bed. A very pale blue with a shadow stripe. They looked like silk.

Undoing her robe, she got quickly into bed. She was wearing a green and white striped nightie. It was cotton as she believed in practical rather than frivolous nightwear. Middle-aged, she thought, wondering what kind of nightgown the feminine Deborah More would wear if it was her honeymoon.

Silk, she decided, as Matthew switched off his bedside lamp. Real silk, with satin ribbons at neck and waist. Would it be white?

She frowned, then reached across to switch off her own lamp. She decided Deborah would not wear white, more like black. Then a hand snaked across and grasped her wrist and she cried out.

'Goodnight, Emma, dear,' Matthew said softly, squeezing her hand before letting it go.

'G . . . goodnight, Matthew,' she whispered, a heaviness descending upon her. As she thought, he wasn't interested, preferring to save himself for Deborah, perhaps.

Even Ruth said they were lovers. It was a foregone conclusion that he would head straight for Deborah's arms the moment they returned home.

Turning her face to the wall she began to cry,

very quietly, her pillow rapidly becoming damp with tears.

The following day they took the boat to Herm, the nearest habitable island to Guernsey.

Because of the wind they were not able to see it at its best, but did manage to see Shell Beach with its rare shells.

'Unique, this place,' Matthew remarked as they made their way to a small bay, which was almost deserted. They found some shelter from the wind and Emma snuggled into her anorak, admiring the broad sweep of white sand.

'It has one of everything,' he went on, and she turned her chilled face to him. 'One hotel, one shop,' he said quietly, then leaned forward and kissed the tip of her cold nose.

'You're frozen. What would Zara say if you turned into an icicle!' he joked, drawing her arm through his as they plodded on through occasionally lunar-like scenery.

'No traffic. That's one blessing,' Emma commented, her frozen heart thawing a bit as Matthew showed no inclination to let go of her arm.

'Same as Sark. There people go everywhere by cycle or horse. We'll have to learn to wind down, Emma. We're so used to rushing about, tearing around in cars or trains, that we have lost the ability to relax.'

She silently agreed. Then he continued, 'Look at you, for instance.' She opened her mouth in protest, sure he was about to pick holes in her.

'You're tense, overwrought,' he went on, his voice maddingly calm. 'Tired, too. Your eyes are

red and I doubt if you slept much last night. What is
it? The peace and quiet getting you down? Lack of
activity? Boredom?' he suggested, and Emma
wanted to scream.

'It's nothing of any importance,' she lied blithely,
her pride preventing her from telling him.

'Missing Tony, perhaps?' he asked shrewdly, and
she turned to face him, her blue eyes wide with
shock.

'I thought that might be it,' he observed, gazing
down at her stricken face. 'You can't go on grieving
for ever, my dear. Tony would understand.'

'But *you* don't!' she cried wildly. 'You don't
understand!' With a sob, she ran from him but
made little headway in the soft terrain and he
caught up easily.

'Emma, you have to put the past behind you!'
His face was savage, the face of a stranger with its
flaring nostrils and shock of windswept black hair.
'Keep your memories but don't live on them,' he
urged, shaking her.

He did not, could not know that she wasn't living
on memories. Her deep sense of shock, of shame
even, had been because she hadn't once thought of
Tony since her remarriage.

'Yes,' she said dully. 'I've put the past behind
me. And I'm not feeding on memories.'

'Good. That's . . . that's the best medicine,' he
said haltingly, becoming the caring family doctor
again.

Emma seethed inwardly, then shook off his re-
straining hands and plodded stolidly on. The sooner
this honeymoon was over, the better.

After that day, Matthew went out of his way to be kind and reassuring. Emma responded as best she could, unable to tell him that she wasn't grieving for her late husband, she was grieving for this very much alive one!

Together they explored Guernsey thoroughly, taking bus tours of the island and returning later to places that particularly took their fancy. An afternoon at the strawberry farm at St Saviour's was what she enjoyed most, Matthew treating her to an enormous slice of strawberry flan topped with Guernsey cream.

On other days they visited the pottery, the tomato museum, and the occupation museum. Sometimes they simply strolled through the hotel's grounds or sat by the swimming-pool. Matthew swam but Emma had never learned, so she sat dabbling her feet in the pool and watching his powerful body cleave through the water.

He took a lot of exercise, swimming not only in the pool but also in some of the quiet bays they visited. Then in the evenings he went for long walks, sometimes with her, but more often alone.

When they'd had enough of museums and the like, they explored St Peter Port itself, with its VAT-free shops. Emma spent a morning there towards the end of their stay and returned laden with souvenirs for her family and Zara.

For Ruth she bought a couple of tea-towels, since she collected them, and a pretty headscarf illustrated with scenes from Guernsey life. Her mother liked ornaments so that was no problem, but she wasn't sure what to get for Zara.

Matthew didn't know, either, but eventually Emma settled on an island-made souvenir—a Guernsey cow with its yellowish-golden coat and a big smile lighting up its face. It was a stuffed toy, but she didn't think Zara would mind because it was so adorable. And it was small enough to be kept on a mantelpiece. After some thought, Emma got one for herself.

All this time Matthew had remained friendly and helpful, insisting Emma must choose the places she wanted to visit. In fact, he was so helpful that Emma wanted to scream at the top of her voice. If she made an exhibition of herself maybe he would really begin to notice her. As it was she might have been an elderly aunt or sister he was escorting.

When they visited the little chapel at Les Vaux-belets Emma could stand no more. He insisted she must see it from every possible angle and take as many photographs as she wished.

Indeed, it was beautiful, a wonderful tribute to God, made out of shells and pieces of pottery. It still received additions, and Emma marvelled at some of the attractive and unusual pieces used in its construction.

'Seen enough?' Matthew stood at her elbow like a guide. 'There's a little shop over there. Would you like a booklet? Or some postcards?'

With an exasperated sigh, she turned on him, keeping her voice low because the area was crowded with tourists.

'Matthew, please, *please* leave me alone! I don't need a nursemaid, I need a husband!' she hissed, before hurrying down the awkwardly winding steps.

She had to get away. But there was no escape, no one to whom she could turn. If Matthew made just one more helpful comment she would tear her hair out!

She was almost on the main road when a stern-faced Matthew caught up. By now she was ashamed of her outburst. It wasn't his fault he wished she was Deborah.

'Matthew, I apologise,' she began, but the look he turned on her was chilly.

'It's time we were getting back. We have a long walk,' he said stiffly, and a crestfallen Emma fell into step with him.

That night, after a meal eaten in stony silence, Matthew took another of his solitary strolls and Emma went to bed early, having eaten hardly a thing.

It was all over before it had even begun. Their marriage was a mistake and not even their love for Zara could cement it together.

CHAPTER ELEVEN

EMMA WAS still awake when Matthew returned from his solitary stroll, though it couldn't have been solitary because she distinctly heard his chuckle, his deep voice as he called, 'Goodnight.'

Then the bedroom door opened and his dominating presence filled the darkened room. Emma tensed, wondering if he would make some hurtful remark, but he didn't.

She heard him go through to the bathroom, then she relaxed, trying to untense her jangled nerves. Was it always to be like this? she wondered. Two strangers sharing a room, sharing a sham of a marriage.

She had only herself to blame if she didn't like it. She knew the terms of the marriage before the ceremony—a mother for Zara, an unpaid second housekeeper and cook for the doctor.

She must have been incredibly gullible to believe that there would be more to their marriage than that. Matthew coming to her bed that morning had been a bonus born out of his physical need. She was available and willing, God help her, and even doctors were human.

She blushed a little at the memory. Matthew was a considerate and tender lover and she could have asked for no better. For that one occasion she must give thanks and be satisfied.

But if only he had come to her in love! She sat up and glanced about her wildly. She could see the glimmer of light from under the bathroom door and was tempted to hammer on it, tell Matthew she needed him.

Look at me! she wanted to tell him. I'm your wife, I love you!

Wouldn't that be something? A weary smile crossed her face as reason prevailed. She could do nothing of the kind. Basically she was a shy person. No way could she throw herself at a man, even if he was her husband.

She sank back against the pillows. Finding them hot and uncomfortable, she was punching the top one savagely when Matthew returned.

It seemed like hours before she dropped off, listening to the even, regular breathing that came, after a while, from the other bed. Matthew Scofield, I hate you, she thought before slipping into a light doze.

Some slight noise or movement awakened her. Matthew was climbing into her bed, pushing her gently to one side.

Indignant, she sat up. 'Are you cold?' she asked, her voice chilly. 'Ring down for a hot water bottle.'

'I don't need a hot water bottle. I have a wife to warm me.' Matthew's voice was calm, his tone suggesting she was addle-headed and needed even obvious facts explained to her.

'Matthew Scofield, I will not be used!' she began, but he snuggled closer and all thoughts of resistance flew from Emma's mind.

She clung to him in desperation, as if this was to be the last time, as if they were shortly to part.

'Emma,' he murmured, and she caught her breath in wonder at the yearning in his voice. She moved restlessly against him. She so wanted, so loved him, but yet . . .

Their lips met, broke apart and met again. Then he rained gentle kisses upon her brow, her nose, the softness of her throat, and an agonised moan broke from her.

I love him, she thought as she moulded herself to his dark, muscular length. If I come in love it doesn't matter that I'm only a substitute . . .

Perhaps it is an omen, this feeling that we will never lie in one another's arms again, she reflected much later as she lay sleepless. Matthew was asleep now, his passion spent, his arrogant, masculine body tired, at peace.

Her heart swelled with love for him. She eased herself up from where she lay, her head cradled against his shoulder. In the darkness she could not see the strong planes of his face, those expressive, sleepy blue-grey eyes, the dark sweep of his lashes, but she pictured them in her mind.

All these things were part of the man she loved. A tear fell and she sniffed, trying to remember where her hankie was. She didn't want to waken him but . . .

He stirred restlessly and she slipped out of his embrace, finding the hankie under the pillow. She could not control the tears but tried to stifle her sobs in the handkerchief. What a fool he would think her if he caught her crying.

Then strong hands gripped hers and Matthew's soothing voice filled her ears. She clung to him, trying to control her tears and at last succeeded.

'Emma, my dear, don't cry any more. I understand,' he murmured.

She raised her face for his kiss, her lips parted expectantly, eagerly, but he made no move towards her and she tensed, angry with him for not understanding her love and with herself for making the first move. She must wait to be kissed, not expect more than he chose to offer.

'Do you, Matthew? What do you understand?' Her voice was small, withdrawn.

'About Tony. About your needs,' he said, his voice tinged with impatience. 'We both have a need, Emma. We must find our fulfilment in each other.'

Instead of with the people we really love. He didn't say that, but the words hung unsaid over them. Matthew thought she was yearning for Tony and she knew he was yearning for Deborah More.

'You're right,' she agreed, the steadiness of her voice surprising her. 'We need each other. Love doesn't enter into it.'

If bitterness tinged her last sentence he seemed unaware of it, and he squeezed her arm affectionately before turning on his side as best he could. Emma, rejected, lay sleepless until dawn lightened the sky.

They spent the day on the neighbouring island of Sark. An incident there brought home to her even more forcefully the fact that Matthew came to her only in dire need.

After they landed by boat on the island, he stood chatting to another couple who were staying at the same hotel. They were American, and Matthew was explaining some point of interest to them.

Emma wandered over to where the horse-drawn carts waited. She would dearly have loved a ride in one but assumed her husband would want to walk. A tall, fair-haired man hailed her, and she recognised another of the hotel guests.

'We haven't been introduced, but I know you're Mrs Scofield.' He smiled engagingly, and Emma shook his proferred hand, all the time worried in case Matthew should see. They were screened by the horses but he might appear at any minute and she shifted uncomfortably.

'I'm Alan Mepham,' the man went on, and Emma smiled politely.

'Are you taking one of these?' He indicated the conveyances and Emma shook her head.

'I expect we will stroll around. My . . . my husband likes walking.'

'He can't expect you to walk about all day,' Alan insisted, a wide smile on his handsome face. 'Why don't we share one? I'm sure your husband won't mind.'

'I think he would prefer to walk. Really, it's very kind of you, but . . . !

'I wasn't suggesting that he came with us!' he laughed, patting Emma's arm in an over-friendly fashion.

Then, to her horror, she saw Matthew approaching, his step purposeful. She stepped away from Alan, her eyes bleak.

'Excuse me,' my husband is coming,' she said coldly, and the young man shrugged and stood back, a rueful grin on his face.

Emma hardly knew what to say to Matthew. He gave her a quizzical look, and she licked her dry lips.

'You look worried,' he remarked, taking her arm possessively.

As she expected, he chose to walk rather than ride. There were no cars on Sark and they had plenty of room to stroll without worrying about traffic, apart from the horses and one or two people on bicycles.

'I . . . I'm sorry. About that man, I mean,' she said earnestly, once their brisk pace had left the others behind.

'We shall have to slow down, Emma,' he commented. 'It's hilly. We aren't in any particular hurry.'

'No, no, of course we're not.' She slowed down, feeling stupid. 'It's hardly the place to hurry.'

'We have left our other lives behind. No patients, no hospital wards, no health centre,' he pointed out.

Sark wasn't quite of another world. Despite the rocky, hilly terrain and the ever-changing sea so near, there were signs of civilization, of the world they had left behind. Shops, a post office, a pillar-box, cafés, hotels. Yet they were as unobtrusive as it was possible to make them and it was the rugged splendour of the scenery that took the eye.

'Which man?' Matthew asked after a while.

Emma coloured, thinking he had forgotten her

brief apology. 'Oh, it was nothing really. He's staying at our hotel.'

'That fair chap?'

'Mm. He wanted to share a horse and cart with us.'

He smiled. 'I'm surprised he included me in the invitation!'

'He didn't,' she felt forced to admit, and Matthew's smile broadened.

'Can't blame him, I suppose. You look very fetching in that blue silky thing.'

Feeling absurdly pleased that he'd noticed her new dress, Emma thanked him and then said how sorry she was about Alan Mepham.

'Oh? Got a name, has he?' Matthew asked, his normally sleepy-looking eyes suddenly alert, and Emma flushed. 'Why do you keep on about him?' he persisted.

'I thought you might mind—about him chatting me up, I mean. Tony . . . Tony used to work himself into a jealous rage!' With an effort she kept her tone light, but Tony's rages had been frightening.

'I shan't, if that's what's bothering you,' he said, equally lightly. 'I have no reason to be jealous. It doesn't matter to me.'

Emma felt sick. He need not have put it so baldly. Yet he was being honest. He spoke no more than the truth when he said it didn't matter to him. She could flirt with all the guests and Matthew wouldn't turn a hair. He wasn't interested, did not love her and therefore there was no point in him being jealous.

Once more her invidious position was driven home to her, and it hurt. It was as if each word he uttered drove a stake into her heart. He did not care for her other than as a woman to whom he could turn in the night.

All hope gone, Emma became quiet and subdued for the rest of the day. That night Matthew did not come to her bed and she supposed he was too weary. He had no need of her, but her needs remained the same. She so wanted him to take her in his arms, comfort and soothe her, murmur soft, silly words of love. No more than that. But he did not come, and the night was long and cold.

They were back in Calbridge early the next evening. It was a lovely evening and Emma strolled by herself in the big, rather wild garden of King's House.

Zara was still with her grandfather and would not be returning for another two days. It gave Emma time to unwind, to adjust to her new role, that of wife to a GP.

She would miss the health centre. And the hospital, come to that. But Matthew had promised she could still visit the old folk and she was looking forward to seeing Mrs Drummond again, not to mention the moth-eaten ginger cat!

Matthew was preoccupied during the short flight back to the mainland, and once back in his own home he reverted to being the family doctor. Almost as soon as he arrived, he was on the telephone to Dr Partington, enquiring after some of the patients.

When Emma shyly asked if she could help in any

way, he had regarded her sadly, then shook his
head, suggesting that she find her way about the
house, get her bearings. That was the last thing
Emma wanted. The walls closed in upon her and
she escaped to the garden.

It badly needed attention but she wasn't much of
a gardener. Her mother had green fingers and she
was sure Matthew wouldn't mind if her parents
came for an extended visit. He would probably be
relieved, glad that Emma had guests with whom to
occupy herself, keep her from getting in his way.

He would not be returning to duty until the
following Monday but later, as she was preparing
their supper in the well-equipped kitchen, he came
in, already dressed in his dark business suit.

'Sorry, Emma, but Steve Dutton's had an accident and Dr Bhunjun's on holiday, so they're
rather short. I've promised to make one or two
visits.'

'Oh! Stephen . . . is he hurt?' She liked Stephen
Dutton. He had taken her out only the once the
previous spring, but they had remained friends and
he'd been far kinder to her than Matthew ever was.

'Nothing serious. A fractured humerus, some
bruising and lacerations.' His tone was cool as if he
didn't care. Anyway, he wasn't the kind of man to
show his feelings, as Emma knew only too well.

She swallowed. 'Good. I . . . I'm glad he isn't
hurt. Will you—I don't suppose you want supper?'
She answered her own question and did not need
his regretful shake of the head.

'I've eaten enough to last me the rest of the
month! You have yours and I'll get a cold snack

when I come in. Don't wait up!' he called from the hall. Then the heavy front door slammed and Emma was alone in the big house.

Supper no longer interested her and she made do with a cheese sandwich. Mrs Fillery had been coming in just to dust and tidy, and had left the fridge and freezer well-stocked for their return.

She wouldn't be coming again until Monday and Emma was glad. The woman was too perceptive and utterly devoted to 'young Dr Matthew' as she called him. She would know at once that all was not well with the marriage and Emma hoped she wasn't a gossip.

Later, as she prepared for bed, the phone shrilled and she raced downstairs in her new pink nightie. It must be Matthew letting her know he was on his way home. How thoughtful of him. A warm glow rose within her. Darling Matthew.

Deborah More's husky voice soon dispelled any warm feelings she might have been entertaining towards him.

'Matthew isn't in?' Deborah sounded surprised, almost shocked, that he should leave his new bride so soon, and Emma defensively muttered something about emergencies.

The throaty chuckle at the other end of the line emphasised Deborah More's total disbelief. 'He isn't due back until Monday! I'm sure we can cope another day or so. Ask him to ring me when he gets in, will you? He knows the number.'

She rang off and Emma was left staring foolishly at the receiver.

Matthew knows the number. Of course he does.

Weren't they lovers until recently? No doubt they would resume their relationship once Matthew was back at work, she mused dully, an ache beginning over her left eye. It matched the one in her heart.

Deborah must be right about the work-load, as well. She said they could manage without Matthew until Monday and she ought to know.

Where was he then? Emma closed her tired eyes. As he said, he probably *was* doing a few visits. But were they necessary, and did he need to stay out half the night?

No, he had offered, chosen to do them. Anything to get away from his new wife. Angry rather than sad, Emma slowly made her way upstairs.

It was just after eleven when she switched off the light and must have been well past midnight when she heard Matthew return. She hadn't slept and, mindful of her promise to Dr More, she crept down, her bare feet sinking into the thick carpet.

He was slumped in his favourite chair by the fire. His expression was anything but welcoming when he glanced up and saw her.

Uncertainly, Emma gabbled her message about ringing Deborah More. From the look on his face she wondered what she had done wrong this time, and she sadly turned to go. But Matthew's deep voice halted her in her tracks.

'He's going to be all right. It wasn't serious, as I suspected.'

'Who?' Her surprise must have been convincing, for it was his turn now to look uncertain.

'Why, Steve Dutton. Wasn't that why you've

been lying in wait for me? I know you've grown fond of him', he accused, his tone bitter.

'I . . . he reminds me of Tony!' was all Emma could say.

'So you said. That makes a bonus then, doesn't it?'

He sprang up and Emma scurried away, wondering what he had in mind.

She need not have worried. When she risked a quick glance over the banisters she saw him using the hall telephone.

Ashamed of herself for listening, she heard Matthew's chuckle and his words. 'Deb! Lovely to hear your voice again. Is it all fixed up?' He lowered his tone, and Emma crept away.

She didn't want to hear any more. It was obvious they were arranging a meeting. A pseudo-emergency, perhaps?

Dry-eyed she got back into the bed. Unfortunately, it was a double one and there would be no escape if Matthew should want her. But with Deborah so conveniently near, she doubted that Matthew would trouble her again.

CHAPTER TWELVE

MATTHEW must have slept on the settee, for the pillows beside Emma were undisturbed when she awoke next morning.

She got a shock when she saw the time. But there was some excuse for oversleeping, for it must have been nearly dawn when she finally dropped off. Unrefreshed and aching, she had a leisurely bath, dressed, then started the unpacking she ought to have attended to before.

She didn't feel like breakfast, though a cup of coffee would have been welcome. That meant going downstairs and facing the bear-like Matthew, so she was prepared to do without her coffee for the time being. She simply could not face him in her present uncertain state.

She hadn't understood the remark about Stephen Dutton last night. It couldn't be that Matthew was jealous, could it? No, he didn't care one way or the other. He was a bit put out because he thought she preferred Stephen.

As she unpacked her cotton nightie, the one she'd worn the first time she and Matthew made love, a wave of longing overcame her and she clutched the garment tightly, trying to hold back the tears. Almost reverently, she folded it, smoothed out its creases, then put it to one side, away from the main pile of washing.

Washing. She smiled ruefully as item after item appeared. Matthew's as well as her own. Socks galore, pants, shirts . . .

Each item of his she stroked wistfully before adding it to the pile. At this rate she would be laundering all week. Fortunately the house was well supplied with domestic gadgets, even a tumble-dryer, which was something Emma had never had before.

Doing the chores would keep her out of Matthew's way. I must keep out of Matthew's way, she repeated silently as, much later, she made her way downstairs with a great pile of dirty linen.

She needn't have worried. Her husband was nowhere to be seen, but there was a note on the hall table by the telephone.

She scanned it as she passed. 'Visiting. Back for late lunch'.

With a sigh of relief she put her burden into the linen basket in the utility room, which was an extension built onto the kitchen. Late lunch could mean any time between one-thirty and three, so she rustled up a salad for herself once the clothes were on the rotary clothes line, and sat in Matthew's study nibbling at the sparse meal, her thoughts with him, wherever he might be.

Dr Partington phoned, and she was trying to sound bright and sparkling when Matthew returned. She glanced up as he hovered in the hall, her false laughter fading. 'Here's Matthew now. I'll hand you over,' she told the old doctor, and with a curt nod Matthew took the receiver, their fingers touching briefly.

Pulling her hand away, Emma almost ran back to the study, guiltily aware that she ought not be in there at all and certainly should not have been eating there. She was washing up her plates when Matthew entered the kitchen a little later.

'What do you want to eat?' she asked diffidently. 'There's some salad, ham, fresh bread rolls. Or I could cook you an . . .'

Irritably, he waved her to silence. 'It's all right. I've eaten.'

Colour burned in her cheeks. 'I will not be waved down like that! I'm not your receptionist now!' she snapped, causing him to spin round, his face registering his astonishment.

'I suppose you lunched with Deborah,' she went on, unable to stop now. 'Well, I hope it choked you!' she finished, horrified at her own spitefulness.

Matthew threw back his head and laughed, and Emma felt small. He had no business poking fun at her. Lunching with the other woman, then coming back here to taunt her!

'As a matter of fact, Ruth bought me a cheese and tomato sandwich!' he chuckled, and Emma grew redder.

'She seems to think I was starved in Guernsey,' he went on, and Emma managed a tiny smile before carrying on with her chores.

Savagely she thumped the dish-mop against the plate. She had played right into Deborah More's hands, letting Matthew see he'd married a jealous, suspicious shrew. Now he had a valid excuse for finding solace in Deborah's arms. He could truly say 'my wife doesn't understand me', for she did not.

Matthew was an enigma, a closed book to her. She hoped he would find happiness with Deborah. No, she didn't. That wasn't what she hoped at all! She . . . .

'You will wash the design right off that plate,' Matthew said gently, prising the dish-mop from her steely grip.

She opened her mouth to harangue him again, then closed it firmly. She wouldn't be a shrew. If he was happy with Deborah, so be it.

'No comment?' he asked quizzically and, ashamed of her earlier outburst, Emma shook her head.

He lifted a hand to touch her golden hair, then let it fall again. 'I've told Father we will pick up Zara tomorrow morning. She's anxious to come back.'

Emma raised her dark blue eyes to his, their colour deepened by her inner sadness.

'Your eyes are almost violet today,' Matthew observed huskily.

She shrugged. 'Change of climate, perhaps?' She was hurt that he wanted his daughter back a day earlier than arranged, yet wouldn't it be a relief? She could fuss over the girl, take her out, anything to take her mind off Matthew and Deborah locked in each other's arms somewhere.

'That will be lovely,' she said, with something approaching her old enthusiasm.

'What will, Emma?' His tone was patient.

'Zara coming home early,' she said, equally patiently. 'I . . . I'll just pop up and see that everything is ready for her,' she muttered, hurriedly finishing the last of the dishes.

Then she remembered Tony's rocking-chair, now firmly settled in Zara's room. If Matthew had waited, Mrs Fillery would have returned before Zara and *she* could have dusted and tidied the room instead of Emma.

Yet nothing would be gained by running away. The chair—and her memories—must be faced sooner or later.

Matthew followed her to the foot of the stairs. Then the telephone rang and she heard his terse, 'I'm on my way,' as she paused on the second stair.

Their eyes met as he replaced the receiver. 'One of my old ladies is dead. No apparent cause,' he said briefly. 'See you later.'

He was gone before she could ask the patient's name, and Emma nibbled her lower lip, wondering which old lady it was. But he had so many old ladies. Hundreds, probably.

She could not possibly have met them all in the few months she'd been at the centre. There was crabby Miss Butler, but she was Dr Partington's. Mrs Drummond . . .

Then Emma remembered Miss Law, a lady of about seventy who was suffering from advanced cancer. Could it be her? The health visitor kept an eye on her and she already had a voluntary visitor. That was why Emma had been only the once. Yet the patient had stayed in her mind long afterwards. However, if she had died, the cause was obvious.

What about Miss Spenlow? She was always complaining of odd symptoms.

Emma's head buzzed. So many of them, and all with problems. One day she, too, would be old and she hoped she faced old age and approaching death with the courage shown by most of Matthew's patients.

Ought she to call on Miss Law, just in case? she wondered. Matthew wouldn't like her interfering. And if it wasn't her, what excuse could she offer Miss Law for visiting?

In the end she rang Ruth Evans at the health centre and learned that Ruth knew nothing of a death. After a few minutes' conversation, a perplexed Emma rang off.

It was only later that suspicions began to grow. Was this the excuse Matthew and Deborah had concocted on the telephone? Matthew had asked if it was all arranged, she recalled.

Angrily, she shook herself. She was wicked to harbour such thoughts. Of course it was an emergency. The fact that Ruth knew nothing of it was not necessarily significant . . .

Rain pelted the window-panes, and Emma was peering out at the gathering dusk for the umpteenth time when she saw his car crawl up the long drive. Determined not to let her stupid suspicions show, Emma welcomed him with a warm smile.

An answering smile flickered across his full mouth, but his eyes remained bleak, wary even.

'How . . . how is everything?' she asked breathlessly, taking his coat and methodically hanging it up.

He shook rain-water from his hair before re-
plying. 'Fine except for the weather. The car kept
faltering. Thought I shouldn't make it back at one
point.'

'No, no! I meant the old lady! The one who died,'
Emma said, exasperated at what she considered his
stupid preoccupation with the car. Couldn't he
remember why he was called out?

'I'm off duty now, Emma. I dislike talking shop,'
he said briefly, before disappearing into the downstairs cloakroom, leaving an ashen-faced Emma to
become a victim of her own vivid imagination.

Why wouldn't he talk about it? Why? Emma
clenched and unclenched her fists, her thoughts in
turmoil. She could understand and sympathise with
his reluctance to talk shop, but he could at least
have told her the lady's name. Couldn't he? Of
course he could!

Indignation overcame her, and she had half a
mind to bang on the cloakroom door and demand
an explanation. Instead, she wandered disconsolately into the kitchen to check on his meal. She'd
prepared chicken Kiev, having learned that Mrs
Fillery often gave him that.

As he was so fault-finding where she was concerned, he would probably not like her way of
preparing the dish, but she knew he would eat it,
anyway. Zara had told her he never wasted food
and usually ate anything that was placed before
him.

Zara, who was a faddy eater, and Emma herself
with her bird-like appetite, could learn a lot from
Matthew! Smiling at the thought, Emma carried

the tray through to the panelled dining-room.

Matthew was standing with his back to her, hands thrust into trouser pockets, dark head bent. There was a bottle of whisky and a glass in front of him on the side-table, and Emma paused in the doorway, afraid to disturb him.

No matter what she did, it was wrong in Matthew's eyes. Yet she tried so hard in her anxiety to please him. The ghosts of Tony and Celia hung between them as she entered the room, disturbing Matthew, who glanced around in surprise.

'If you dare tell me you have already eaten, I shall scream,' she said calmly, placing the plates on the table.

After a moment's hesitation, Matthew came to sit opposite, whisky glass in hand.

'This smells appetising,' he commented, before finishing his drink.

He looked tired, even his hair hung down rather limply, and Emma fought down the urge to flick it back. Her heart yearned for him, yet he was as far from her as ever.

To his credit, he finished every scrap of the meal, though he refused the lemon mousse.

'Couldn't eat another bite,' he assured her, leaning back and gazing at her from under half-closed lids.

'Was that your second dinner?' Emma asked shrewdly, and Matthew flushed.

Then he gave a curiously boyish grin. 'Does it show?'

'I appreciate you have a big frame to fill but I

don't think two dinners a day are good for your digestion!' Emma kept her voice light. She would *not* nag. But it was so terribly unfair. How could she cope? If he was going to eat at Deborah's he might as well sleep and live there as well!

Her eyes became a stormy, deep, violet-blue, and Matthew leaned forward and chuckled.

'It isn't funny!' she snapped, rising to her feet. 'I hate you, Matthew Scofield!'

She stormed out, sure her heart would break into a million pieces. She hoped the chicken Kiev would give him indigestion!

If she hoped he would follow her to the bedroom and offer an explanation or even an apology, her hopes were dashed, and bitterness washed over her. Matthew was openly carrying on with Deborah, yet it never occurred to him that his wife might mind! The man was no better than a gigolo!

In the end she decided to sleep in Zara's room. Then she remembered the rocking-chair. No, she couldn't sleep there.

Of course there were spare bedrooms. Three, in fact, but there was no linen on the beds and the rooms hadn't been aired. It was cowardly, anyway. She must face Matthew's wrath tonight, if he decided to sleep in his own bed.

She was sitting quietly in the bedroom, the door open, when the front door bell rang, and she heard Matthew answer it.

It was Deborah More. Emma went on to the landing. She couldn't see without being seen, but there was no mistaking Deborah's husky tones.

'Darling Matthew!' she trilled. 'It's all fixed!'

Emma went white. Even more so at the unmistakable sound of a kiss. Her position was untenable. No way could she stay here under the same roof as her husband and his girlfriend.

But what could she do, where could she go? There was nowhere and no one to go to. She had given up her room after her marriage. She had no friends in the vicinity. Her parents lived too far away for her to go that night. Beside, she was too weary and too upset to drive.

No, she was trapped. While Matthew and Deborah enjoyed an evening by themselves downstairs, she was imprisoned upstairs! In a panic, she tiptoed along the landing to Zara's room—and found herself face to face with the old rocking-chair. She glared at it, then automatically went over and smoothed its cushion. Thankfully, its spell was broken. She no longer saw Tony sitting there waiting for her to fetch his slippers. She saw just what anyone else would see—a family heirloom, an ancient rocking-chair.

She stretched out on the bed and closed her eyes. And then it came to her. She was being a coward. Was she some weak, mouse-like creature to scurry into a cupboard every time someone hurt her?

The answer was a most emphatic no! Emma's blood boiled and she sat up, willing her tired brain to formulate a plan. She would show Deborah More a thing or two.

But when, freshly made up and wearing her new silky blue dress, Emma ventured downstairs, they were nowhere to be seen. Puzzled, because she hadn't heard the front door, Emma went from room to room, saving Matthew's study for last.

Her hand on the doorknob, she paused. Ought she to knock? It *was* his private sanctum. No! It was her house as much as his now.

Determination in every line of her, she turned the knob and advanced, false smile at the ready. But the room was empty and Emma felt deflated. She so wanted to confront Deborah, play the great hostess, let her see it was Emma's home now, that *she* was wife-in-residence, no matter if Deborah was his girlfriend.

By the time she thought of the garden it was too late. They were standing in the rear garden, some distance from her, and Matthew was kissing Deborah's brow.

Courage deserted Emma. She couldn't confront them, she couldn't. Her pride was all she had to cling to now.

Bleakly, she watched as they strolled back, but they did not return to the house. To her surprise they went around the side, where Deborah's white car was parked.

Disconsolately, she watched Deborah drive away. No doubt they had been fixing their next meeting.

Matthew caught sight of Emma as she paused, uncertain whether to return to the house or stroll around the garden. Although the ground was damp, the rain had cleared. But she really needed a jacket as the nights were starting to develop that autumnal nip.

'Emma!' His deep voice made her name sound

beautiful, she mused. With a kind of detachment, she watched his approach.

'Emma, you'll catch cold.' His voice was tender, concerned even, and Emma's lip curled.

He must believe her to be naive! That act didn't fool her one little bit.

'You don't care one way or the other!' she snapped, startling him into halting a few feet away.

'I thought I did care,' he said gently, a half-smile on his lips. 'Deborah sends her regards,' he added.

That did it. Emma exploded. That remark was all she needed to prove her point. How could he! How dare he!

Eyes bright with temper and unshed tears, she ran up to him and began to beat him with her fists. 'I loathe you, Matthew Scofield!' she cried. 'I wish you joy of Deborah More. You . . . you can have the whole house to yourselves next time—I'm leaving!'

Quickly he caught her wrists and when she couldn't hit him she began kicking instead, until he half-carried, half-dragged her to the garage and dumped her on the chair.

Face flushed and eyes ablaze, she lunged at him again but his arms effectively prevented another attack. And anyway, she had lost interest in hurting him now.

'From the way you are behaving, one might diagnose jealousy,' he said, laughter in his voice, and Emma glared.

'One would be wrong then! One couldn't care

less,' she assured him, defiant to the last.

'Funny, I could have sworn that outburst was prompted by jealousy.'

'It wasn't!' she said truculently, and he began to laugh.

She glared at him while the tears ran unheeded down her cheeks. Oh, how she loved him! If only . . . .

'I wish I didn't love such a jealous woman,' Matthew said mournfully, leaning against the work-bench as he surveyed her.

'I'm sure Deborah has no reason for jealousy,' Emma's voice was stiff and cold. She mustn't let him hurt her pride again.

'Deborah? Was I talking about Deborah?' He frowned. 'I could have sworn the jealous woman I love is called Emma Scofield.'

'W . . . what?' Surely he was joking, mocking her? Why, he had never loved her! She was just a convenient woman to mother Zara.

'Is there something the matter with your hearing?' he enquired mildly, those sleepy eyes devouring her. 'I could arrange for the health visitor to syringe your ears if you wish!'

Then he opened his arms almost hesitantly, his gaze uncertain now. But there was no uncertainty about the way in which Emma ran to him, to find herself enfolded in his strong arms, her heart pressed against his.

'Emma, my love. I didn't know you were jealous of Deborah,' he murmured. 'She means nothing to me.'

Emma swallowed nervously. How she wanted to

believe him—but she could not deny the evidence of her own eyes.

'You were together in the house—and the garden. Kissing. I saw you. Oh, Matthew!' She clung to him all the harder, wondering if her dreams of love were going to be broken yet again.

'It was a kiss of hello and goodbye. Bon voyage, pleasant journey. Hope you get on well in America and so on.'

'America?' she echoed, pulling away so that her eyes could search his face.

'Deb's got the post in the USA that she has always wanted. She's a talented girl.'

There was no mistaking the sincerity in his voice, the love in those big, blue-grey eyes. The intensity of his gaze caused Emma to curl her toes, desire and love shooting through her like a flame, from head to toe.

'You *did* love her, though, didn't you?' she asked wistfully, as they strolled hand in hand back to the house.

'I was fond of her,' he admitted. 'We were lovers, yes, there's no point in denying that. But I never intended marriage. She knew that, Emma. I didn't string her along, then dump her when a certain sad-eyed, golden girl came into my life!'

He stopped, to gaze into her eyes. 'You must believe that, Emma. Once you came, my interest in Deborah vanished. It had been on the wane for sometime. For both of us,' he assured her. 'I wanted a real mother for Zara,' he went on, pushing open the back door and locking it behind them. 'I wanted a real wife, too,' he said wistfully.

'Who fed you?' she burst out suddenly.

Matthew just stared, and Emma hurried on, 'The chicken Kiev was your second dinner. You admitted it.'

'I was joking,' he confessed, with a grin. 'I thought I might make you just a tiny bit jealous if I pretended someone else was feeding me, too!'

Relief overwhelmed her, but there was still one question unanswered. 'What about your old lady? I . . . I thought when you said one of your patients was dead that it was just an excuse to spend some time with Deborah,' she admitted, hoping he would not hold her stupid jealousy against her.

'Emma!'

Aghast at the steel in his voice, she opened her mouth to tell him she didn't mean it, but found her lips imprisoned by his.

It was a long while afterwards that she heard about the patient, a lady she had never met, a Miss Miller. She had died from natural causes but because she hadn't been ill and seldom attended the surgery, her death was unexpected. By then Emma would have believed him if he had said a three-headed Martian had landed in the back garden!

As she lay happily in his arms, after their stormy love-making, she knew that whatever had gone before, a whole new life stretched ahead of them both. For Zara, too, there would be a new beginning.

Perhaps one day, a new brother or sister for Zara, as well, for Matthew had found a real wife and she had found a real husband.